M000202857

To Katheron

Enjoy the book

Amy Scott

MY LIFE MY CHOICE

"To say goodbye is to die a little"
Raymond Chandler

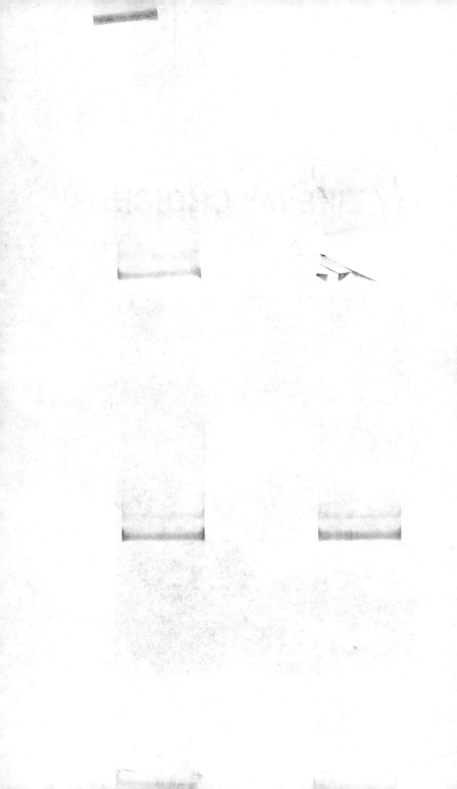

MY LIFE MY CHOICE

GARY SMITH

gatekeeper press

Columbus, Ohio

My Life My Choice

Published by Gatekeeper Press
2167 Stringtown Rd, Suite 109
Columbus, OH 43123-2989
www.GatekeeperPress.com

The cover design and editorial work for this book are entirely the product of the author. Gatekeeper Press did not participate in and is not responsible for any aspect of these elements.

ISBN (hardcover): 9781642379211

Dedicated to:

Mary and Cesare Sategna
My grandparents

ACKNOWLEDGEMENTS

Writing the synopsis and proofreading:	Ken Meirovitz
Proofreading:	Andrea Rezzonico
Proofreading:	Jane Olson
Photographs:	Gary Smith

CONTENTS

Acknowledgements vii
Chapter 1 1
Chapter 2 7
Chapter 3 13
Chapter 4 19
Chapter 5 25
Chapter 6 31
Chapter 7 37
Chapter 8 43
Chapter 9 49
Chapter 10 55
Chapter 11 61
Chapter 12 65
Chapter 13 69
Chapter 14 75
Chapter 15 79
Chapter 16 85

Chapter 17 91

Chapter 18 95

Chapter 19 101

Chapter 20 107

Chapter 21 113

Chapter 22 117

Chapter 23 123

Chapter 24 127

Chapter 25 133

Chapter 26 137

Chapter 27 143

Chapter 28 147

Chapter 29 153

Chapter 30 159

Chapter 31 165

Chapter 32 169

Chapter 33 175

Chapter 34 181

Chapter 35 185

Chapter 36 191

Chapter 37 197

Chapter 38 203

Chapter 39 209

Chapter 40 215

Chapter 41 221

Chapter 42 227

Chapter 43 233
Chapter 44 239
Chapter 45 245
Chapter 46 249
Chapter 47 253
Chapter 48 259
Chapter 49 263
Chapter 50 269
Chapter 51 275
Chapter 52 281
Chapter 53 287
Chapter 54 291
Chapter 55 295
Chapter 56 301
Chapter 57 305
Chapter 58 309
Chapter 59 315

Chapter 1

IT WAS EARLY Friday morning, and I was driving to Florence from my home in Muriaglio, Italy. I had left the village about three hours before and was on the Autostrada near Viareggio, almost to Pisa. It was a clear spring morning, and the Tuscan light shining on the sea was beautiful. The five-hour drive to Florence gave me plenty of time to think of all the ways my life had changed since my wife and I discovered my grandfather's village: Muriaglio.

Muriaglio is a small village approximately forty kilometers north of Turin Italy near the start of the Aosta Valley. Several years back, my third wife and I had found it on our twenty-fifth wedding anniversary. To our surprise, we were greeted by a family member whom I didn't know existed.

I started studying Italian, sold my electrical contracting business, and began going back every year to visit. I can't explain the deep emotional ties I have to Muriaglio; only to say walking into that village gave me a sense of belonging I had been searching for my entire life.

A few years after finding the village, my wife died in a car crash, and I began living most of the year in Muriaglo. Today I am driving to Florence, Italy, to keep a promise I made to Maria Sategna.

Maria was thirty-five years old. She was about five feet eight inches tall with long black hair and dark, seductive eyes. She wasn't thin, but was not heavy, with the little extra weight made use of in all the right places. Twice she has helped me out of some tough spots. We met about five years ago when I was studying Italian in Florence. I rented one of her apartments while in school for a month. I met Cindy O'Brian in class and fell in love. Cindy found herself in a bit of trouble, and Maria helped Cindy and me get out of Italy while being chased by the FBI, terrorists, and Home-land Security. Then again, eighteen months ago, she hid a friend and me in one of her apartments, risking retribution from the Moretti crime family for doing so. I owe her a great debt for her help over the years, and today I'm on my way to make a payment.

I feel very close to Maria and would do anything for her. I know she would like the relationship to be more, but she has accepted the fact that I'm deeply in love with Cindy O'Brian.

Cindy was married with children and devoted to her family. We acknowledged our love for each other and didn't pursue it any further. Two years ago, she turned up in Muriaglio. Her husband divorced her for another woman, and she came to Italy looking for me. We spent the most perfect six months together. During this time, she released a number one record album. While on tour, she attracted a stalker/serial killer and was abducted and almost killed in

Italy near Muriaglio. It was very traumatic for her and her family, especially her ex-husband. He had a lot of remorse and regrets, and he asked her to come home. She left and went back home in hopes of putting her marriage back together for her children.

That is the status of my life; in love with a woman I haven't had contact with for eighteen months, living alone in Italy most of that time, and on my way to spend the weekend with a woman who would love our relationship to be more than it is. It sounds like the life of a writer, and it is. My name is Warren Steelgrave. I wrote my first book, *The Willing*, about escaping Italy with Cindy O'Brian, and it became a best seller. I just sent my third novel to my editor, and I'm off to Florence for the weekend.

I always get confused as to which part of town you can drive in, so I park in a parking garage near the airport and take a taxi. I get off the autostrada and make my way to the long-term parking, *Sosta Lunga P3*, near the airport. I have never been to Maria's apartment, and I'm very impressed as I get out of the taxi. The apartment building is near the Piazzale Michelangelo. It is not an overly large building; a pale yellow, and very ornate. I walk up the marble steps to the large wooden carved door. To the right of the door is the list of the apartments by name. There are only nine apartments in the building. I find Maria's name and push the button next to it. As I wait, I get a feeling I'm being watched. I hope Maria doesn't have a jealous boyfriend.

"*Pronto*"

"Ciao, Maria. It's Warren."

"Ciao Warren. Come up to the third floor."

Just then, I heard the door unlock. I opened it, entered the marbled entrance, and started up the stairs with my small weekend bag. I started up the last flight of stairs and standing at the top is Maria. She is wearing a white cotton blouse pulled just off the shoulders and tucked into the waist of a red skirt with a wide black belt and black flats for shoes. Her long dark hair had soft curls hanging over one shoulder. She had very little makeup on, and simple but expensive jewelry. Looking up at her confident and seductive eyes, I thought I was looking at a fashion magazine cover.

"Ciao, Maria"

"Ciao, Warren, come stai?"

"Va bene! E tu?"

I could tell by her little smile she was happy at my gawking at her looks.

"I have our day planned, Warren. Come and put your bag away and have a coffee. I will explain, hope you don't mind."

"Not at all Maria I'm yours for the weekend."

Reaching the top of the stairs, I sat down my bag and gave her a big hug and a kiss on both cheeks. God, she smelled good. It felt so good to hold a woman in my arms; it had been a while. Picking up my bag, I followed her into the apartment and to my room. The room was small but well-appointed. It had an antique bed and armoire and a window that looked out over the city of Florence.

"Make yourself comfortable, Warren. I will go prepare the coffee."

I unpacked and freshened up a little in the bathroom and needed to shave again. I changed my shirt and walked to the kitchen. Maria was just pouring the coffee.

"You have a beautiful apartment, Maria."

Looking up with that smile of hers, she said, "Thank you, Warren." She handed me an espresso and continued, "Let's have our coffee on the balcony. I remember how much you like views."

I followed her out to the balcony. The view was stunning. We sat at a small table on the balcony that overlooked the Arno river with a great view of the city and the Ponte Vecchio.

Maria was looking at me with true excitement in her eyes, and said,

"Warren, I want to take you to a small winery near Chianti. After a long walk through the vineyards and some wine tasting of Chianti Classico, they will prepare for us a nice lunch. Also, there is a small village on the way back that I want to show you. After I would like to introduce you to a few local people. I have a good friend who is having a party for a few artists and writers. I wanted to show you off and told them we would come. I hope it is OK?"

"Of course, Maria."

"Let's go."

We finished our coffees, placed the cups in the sink, and headed out the door.

***

Giacomo picked up his cell phone and made a call.

"Pronto."

"Piero, it's Giacomo. Steelgrave has just left with Maria."

"Giacomo, you have to make a connection with him today."

"I understand, Piero. I will stay close and get to him the first chance he is alone."

Chapter 2

MARIA DROVE, AND we headed out of the city. We got on the autostrada headed toward Siena. It was the beginning of spring, and the light this time of year is simply beautiful to paint or photograph with; all the colors seemed brighter somehow. I was enjoying the scenery when Maria broke the silence.

"Warren, how is the family, is everyone good?"

"Everyone is doing well, Maria, and your family?"

"My dad has been ill, but he seems better now."

Somehow, I felt she was going to steer the conversation to Cindy, trying to find out the status of our relationship.

"Warren, I hear your friend Cindy O'Brian has a new album out?"

"I knew it," I said to myself

"I did hear that. I haven't talked to her for a while. I have been busy finishing my last book. There's something I wanted to ask you. The family is coming to Muriaglio in April to have my granddaughter baptized. My grandfather was baptized in the church there, and my daughter thought that it would be special to have her daughter baptized in the same church. It will be only my daughter, her husband, and her mother, my second wife. What I wanted to ask you is; I would like to invite you to stay with me as my guest. After they all leave, we can travel around Northern Italy for a few days."

"I would love that, Warren. Do you have a date?"

"Not yet. Everyone is trying to sync their calendars. So far, the plan is to arrive a day or two before the baptism and leave a day or two after."

"How fun, Warren."

Just then, Maria took the exit off the autostrada and turned left onto Str. Dr. Cortine. After a few miles, she turned down a long gravel road lined with tall Italian Cypress. Before long, we arrived at Casa Sola-Chianti Winery. We pulled up and parked, and as we got out of the car, we were greeted by a man with his two dogs. He extended a hand and said, "Buongiorno, I am Giovanni Peruffo."

"Buongiorno, I am Warren Steelgrave, and may I present Maria Sategna."

"*Piacere*. I know Maria. How is your father?"

"He is doing much better, thank you."

"Shall we start with a walk in the vineyards?"

We both agreed and began walking with Giovanni, the dogs leading the way. It was going to be a pleasant day and not too hot. The air smelled so clean, and the dogs were having so much fun handling their job of leading the way. After about twenty minutes of walking through the vineyards with Giovanni giving us a history of the winery and types of grapes grown, we came to the wine cellar.

The wine cellar was large, with walls made of stone and brick. It had four rooms for barrels of wine with a small corridor going between them; it was incredibly old. We were told the winery had been making wine since 1689. Next, we toured the winemaking process, then we went to the tasting room. In the tasting room, we sampled several of the winery's wines paired with different cheese and salami. I bought a case of their Chianti Classico, and we started to the house for lunch.

We were seated at a small table on a terrace overlooking the vineyards, with a dark blue sky as a backdrop. The table was set with a white tablecloth, some bread, and a bottle of the same wine I had bought. I poured us both a glass and sat back, watching the two dogs play.

"Maria, this is simply beautiful, I am enjoying this a lot."

I looked over at Maria, expecting a response. She was holding her glass of wine close to her face with both hands, peering over the top, looking out over the vineyards with a smile of contentment.

Just then, an elderly-woman, heavy, not obese, wearing a dress and apron; the universal image of a grandmother, approached and set down a plate of antipasti; salami, prosciutto, and melon. After about twenty minutes, she was back with spaghetti. Twenty minutes later, a plate of fried turkey fillets with lemon sauce. Then came a plate of cheeses and finally a plate of cookies and candied strawberries with our coffees.

Lunch took us well into the late afternoon.

Maria looked at her phone and said, "Warren, let's go. I want to take you to the village of San Donato. The shops will be opening soon, and we can walk around and do a little shopping."

"Let's go!"

We got up and said our goodbyes and left. As we turned on to the paved road from the gravel road, I turned to Maria and said, "Are you dating anyone?"

Maria liked where this was headed. She smiled and answered, "No."

"Can you think of a reason someone might follow you?"

This was not what she expected to her response. "No . . . Warren, why do you ask?"

"That car back there, parked on the side of the road, was parked across the street from your apartment."

Maria sighing and shaking her head, said, "It's not me, Warren. You are the only person I know who always has someone following him. What kind of trouble are you in now?"

"Nothing I can think of, Maria."

We continued to the village of San Donato. San Donato was a small village with cobbled streets and fourteenth and fifteenth-century buildings. There, we spent the rest of the afternoon walking the streets and shopping. In the early evening, we found a coffee bar and went in for a snack and a coffee.

"What should we do for dinner, Maria?"

"Are you hungry, Warren? Lunch was it for me today."

"I agree, Maria. What time is the party tonight?"

"It's not until 8:00. We will have time to return to my apartment and freshen up a bit before we go."

We got up and headed back to the car.

"Warren, have you seen that car anymore?"

"No. All foreign cars look alike to me. It was probably two different cars, of the same color."

We got to her car and started back to Florence when I asked, "Tell me a little about who will be at the party tonight?"

"There is not much to tell, Warren. It will be just a small group of friends, maybe twelve. Some are painters. The host of the party is a college professor at the University of Florence. He teaches a class on Renaissance Art, and one writer who wants to meet you."

I didn't reply; I just turned my attention to the passing landscape. Having never gone to college, I always felt at odds with such a group. My view of the world was always different than that of a group of intellectuals. At least with this group, they won't be able to tell how badly I speak American English.

We arrived back at Maria's apartment just before 7:00 p.m. and went in to freshen up.

"I won't be long, Warren, I just want to change my clothes. We have time for a drink before we go. I have an opened white wine in the refrigerator; would you pour me a glass?" Then with a little smile and a chuckle, she continued. "I have gin in the ice-box if you want something stronger."

I found glasses and poured her a glass of wine and made myself a martini and walked out to the deck and sat down.

Looking at the view with a martini in hand, I started thinking of Cindy and all the times we would sit out on my terrace or a balcony somewhere and drink martinis.

Maria appeared and sat down. We talked about the events of the day, finished our drinks, and left for the party.

Chapter 3

WE ARRIVED AT the party by taxi just before 8:00. It was being held at the apartment of Professor Giovanni Biasin, near the University of Florence. It was as she said; it was a small group of intellectuals and artists. The apartment was large, at least three bedrooms. The walls were decorated with paintings, and the furniture was antique. All in all, it had a very comfortable feel.

Before long, I was drinking a martini and feeling comfortable with this group. I walked over and set my drink on a small table and took a seat in a chair next to it. After a time, a writer, Jack, came over and sat in the chair across from me. He introduced himself, and we begin talking about writing styles and favorite authors. He picked up his glass and took a sip of a green liquid.

"What is that you're drinking?" I asked him.

"Absinthe."

"Absinthe, isn't that what Hemmingway's character, Robert Jordan, drank in the book: *For Whom, the Bell Tolls?*"

"That's right; would you like to try some, Warren?"

"Sure. Thanks, Jack. Do I add a little water like in the book?"

"If you want."

I drained my martini glass, and Jack filled it half full of Absinthe from a flask in his pocket. Just as I was adding a little water, Maria walked up.

"Warren, are you sure you want to drink the green devil?"

"I thought I would try just a little."

That was the last I remember about the party.

The sun coming through the window and shining on my face woke me. I lay there a few moments, trying to figure out where I was. God, I was hungover! I was lying on a bed in my underwear, trying to remember what had happened, where I was, and how I got there. I eased myself up to a sitting position on the edge of the bed. I sat there a few moments with my eyes closed, waiting for the room to stop its slow spin. I opened my eyes and saw my clothes folded neatly on a chair in the corner of the room. I got up and managed to get dressed, then eased myself out of the room and into the world.

I started down the hall, and as I got to the kitchen, I realized I was in Maria's apartment. Maria was sitting out on the balcony reading. I walked out and sat on a chair across from her. Setting down her book on the table, she said, "Good morning, Warren."

Before she could go on, I raised a hand to stop her.

"Maria, please let me first apologize. I'm so... so sorry. I hope I didn't embarrass you too much in front of your friends. I don't remember anything after I started talking to a writer, Jack."

Maria took my hand, and with a look somewhere between being sad and disappointment said, "Warren, you were fine. Everyone was impressed with you, and you never got out of line. We left while you could still walk, and you didn't pass out until we got here." After a pause, as she was putting together the right words, she looked at me with deep love and sadness and said, "Warren, you can't drink her out of your life. That kind of love is forever, and there is nothing that will make you forget her and what you had together." Then looking me straight in the eyes said, "I know, believe me, I know."

I didn't know how to respond, so I didn't. After a few seconds, Maria said, "Something to eat, Warren?"

"I don't think I can keep it down right now."

"Let me make a coffee and a toast. I have something you can take, and you'll be fine in an hour."

She got up, leaving me sitting alone with my thoughts. Maria was right; life goes on. Still, I keep thinking about Cindy. When we first fell in love, she was married with children, I wouldn't be part of destroying a family. For the three years we were apart, it was different. She was someone I couldn't have; I would think of her every day. It gave me comfort. The second time coming into my life after her husband left her for another woman, she had no small children; two of them were off to college, and one spent the summer with his dad. We entered a relationship together. This time when she left, I lost something very special that I had, and that is very different than something you couldn't have; it has been very painful. I am not resentful. In fact, I understood why and supported her decision. Still, it is very painful. I remember waking up the first morning with her lying naked next to me, breathing so gently. Lying there looking at the ceiling, thinking of the lyric from the song, *I've Got You Under My Skin,* written by Cole Porter and sung by Frank Sinatra. Like the song, I knew from the start the price I would pay and that it would not end well, but not after only a few months. Just then, Maria appeared.

"Here, Warren, eat this toast and have some coffee, then take this pill and go back to bed for a while. In an hour, you will be fine."

I ate the toast and took the pill. After a few minutes, I got up and took my cup and plate into the kitchen. There I found Maria finishing up the dishes. I washed mine and handed them to her to dry and put away. I reached over and took her hand. She looked up and into my eyes with such need and longing; I took her hand and led her into the bedroom.

We undressed and laid down on the bed. It felt so good to hold Maria in my arms. Looking into her eyes, I said, "Maria, I am not sure you want to get involved with me right now. I am pretty much a damaged person at present."

She gave me a small smile and replied, "I am a big girl, Warren; I can take care of myself."

We made love and fell asleep. After a few hours, I was feeling pretty good. Maria looked over and said, "How do you feel, Warren?"

"Good."

"Do you want to do something today?"

"Yes. How about we go to lunch and walk the city. Better yet, let's have a picnic on the banks of the Arno."

"That would be great, Warren. I know a deli close. We can have them make lunch for us."

If you spend a lot of time alone, you close off emotionally. Your world becomes smaller, and you become a recluse. Being with her yesterday and around people at the party made me realize that was where I was headed. To think I didn't want to come. It was only keeping that promise to her that I came. I realize now how important it is to your well-being to be around people. Today I want to just spend time with her and be around people.

Chapter 4

"*PRONTO?*"

"Piero, it's Giacomo; they are just leaving the apartment. I will follow him, and when I can find him alone or when he leaves to go home, I will approach him."

"Giacomo, it needs to be done today, Mr. Moretti is getting very impatient with us."

"It will be done today."

None of this made any sense to Giacomo. Normally he and Piero would pull up in a car and abduct Steelgrave. That would be so much easier and quicker; Giacomo would do what he was told to do.

Maria and I spent the day together. We laid on the banks of the Arno, enjoying the warm sun, and watching the crew-teams race. The sky is so blue this time of year with large cumulus clouds passing over the Ponte Vecchio.

Warm in the sun yet cool with the need of a sweater in the shade. Near the end of the day, I turned to Maria and said, "It's getting late, Maria, we should go, I still have a long drive."

She smiled and nodded. We walked back to her apartment, and I kissed her goodbye.

"I will see you in a few weeks, Maria, for the baptism?"

Maria smiled. "Yes, Warren. You will email me the date?"

I nodded yes and gave her another kiss and left to go find a taxi. Halfway down the block, a large man approached me.

"Mr. Steelgrave, I have a message for you from Mr. Moretti. He would like to meet with you at his house."

Before I could respond, he handed me a small envelope and continued,

"This is his address and directions you are expected no later than tomorrow."

He then turned and walked away. I opened and looked inside. There was a small hand-written note, it read: *Caro Signor* Steelgrave; I have supplied my address and phone number in case you have forgotten how to get here. Please call at your earliest convenience with a time we can expect your arrival. It was signed, Signor Moretti. At that moment, a taxi pulled up, and I got in.

"*Parli Inglese?*"

"Yes."

"Please take me to the parking garage *Sosta Lunga P3* near the airport. The driver nodded, and we were off. On the way to my car, I wondered to myself why would Mr. Moretti want to see me. I knew better than to say no. Mr. Moretti is head of the Moretti crime family. We have met twice. Once to negotiate the release of a friend's son Tom Marino who was being held for exchange of some Tesla files. Tom got the files to me for safekeeping, and the Moretti family kidnaped Tom to trade for the files. After Tom's release, Mr. Moretti's oldest son was killed while trying to assassinate me at my daughter's wedding. This led to our second meeting. I was concerned that his son's death would lead to retaliation toward my oldest son. Despite being warned about meeting with such a ruthless man, I arranged a meeting.

We met, and I was surprised by the man's intelligence and pragmatism. The meeting took place in his extensive library at his home. I was surprised at the collection of signed first edition books he had read. When I told him of my concerns, he gave a small smile and replied he had the same concerns.

"After all, the attempt on your life was at your daughter's wedding. For many in Italy, such disrespect for the family would not be tolerated. Such back and forth retaliation can get out of hand and is bad for business."

We shook hands, and I thanked him for his time. I left the house surprised that such a ruthless man could earn my respect and had to remind myself of the evil that lurked under the surface. I had been summoned to his house: I was concerned.

I made the drive from Florence to Muriaglio in a little under five hours and got home a little after midnight. I went up the stairs and entered the house and went straight to the bar in the living room and made a martini. I walked out onto the terrace, put on some jazz, and sat down to think. It was very still, and the view looking out over the village with the moon rising was stunning.

My thoughts turned to Maria and the weekend. I hope I didn't open pandora's box. My dad told me never to sleep with a woman that you're not planning a long relationship with. They take it as a commitment. I have always heeded that advice, This weekend, I crossed the line. I didn't

realize how needy I had become. Maria wanting the weekend to be so much more. The day after, the party had me feeling like I had let her down in front of her friends . . . still, I argued with myself it is time that I start to live again, and not keep living like a hermit.

My phone began to buzz; it was my daughter Stephanie.

"Hello"

"Hello, Dad. . . . I'm not disturbing you, am I? I know it's late there."

"Not at all, I was just having a drink before going to bed. What's up?"

"I have the date for the baptism and wanted to check with you if it was OK and not a date of a festival; it seems they have one every couple of weeks."

"Just text me the date, and I will check and get back to you."

"Dad, there is one more thing I want to discuss and didn't feel right putting it in a text." After a long pause as she was struggling with finding the right words, she continued. "The guest list has gotten a little larger. I asked John to be the Godfather . . . , and Cindy to be the Godmother. I hope that's OK. I know the two of you aren't seeing each other, but Dad, she sang at my wedding and saved your life taking a bullet meant for you. If not for her, there would not be a baptism in Italy. I hope you understand."

This was a shock. I sat there thinking through what Stephanie said before I responded. John was my eldest son from my first marriage, her stepbrother. Cindy? All that came to mind was a quote from Raymond Chandler. "There is no trap so deadly as the trap you set for yourself."

"I understand, Stephanie, It's OK. In your text, send a list of guests so I can arrange places for them to stay."

"Thanks, Dad. Goodnight."

"Goodnight, Steph. I love you."

We hung up. I sat thinking, Maria, Cindy, and an ex-wife and maybe two ex-wives at the baptism. Great, just great. I drained what was left of my martini and headed off to bed.

Chapter 5

I AWOKE EARLY, CLOSE to 6:30 a.m., to a clear, chilly
morning. It was the first week of March, and there was
still a lot of snow in the mountains. I checked my phone
and had received a text from Stephanie with a list of attendees.
The date of the baptism was going to be the first weekend in
May. Confirmed attendees were my son John and his wife
Sally, with their twin sons, Cindy and her husband Rick, my
daughter Sherry, John's sister and her husband Robert, and
their two daughters, Stephanie, her husband Jim, and her
mother, Joanne. I looked down the list; at least my first wife
is not on the list, only one ex-wife.

I got up and made the bed, showered, and got dressed.
I made myself a cappuccino and walked out the French
doors onto the terrace. I sat down on the small chair next to
the table Cindy and I had sat at to enjoy the mornings and
our coffee. I picked up my phone and dialed the number
on Signor Moretti's hand-written note.

"Pronto."

I recognized the voice. It was Gino, Signor Moretti's
bodyguard. Gino, as I remember him, was a mountain

of a man, at least 6'6" in height and about 260 pounds, trim with chiseled features and was dressed as if he was the cover photo for GQ magazine. I checked the time on my watch. Gino, it's Warren Steelgrave, you can expect me about 11:30 this morning.

I then called my cousin Gino. He and his wife Maria have a couple of apartments in the village they rent from time to time to Americans in search of their roots.

"Pronto"

"Ciao, Gino. It's Warren. I have some family coming the first weekend in May. Arriving on Thursday and staying seven days. I need places for nine people, can you help me out?"

"Sure, Warren, send me the list by groups that can stay together."

"I will send it now. Thank, Gino."

I hung up and sent Stephanie's list with a note that Sherry's family would be staying with me. I grabbed my coat and headed out the door on my way to Cremona and the home of Signor Moretti.

It took me just under three hours to get to the home of Signor Moretti, not bad considering the traffic around Milan. I drove down the very long cypress-lined driveway. The driveway ends in a circular court with a fountain in the middle. I drove into the court and parked in front of the front door. I got out and rang the front-door-bell, and shortly the door opened. Gino was standing there, motioning me to enter. He was as well-groomed and as big as ever, complete with a slight bulge under the coat: his gun. I walked in, and Signor Moretti was standing at the base of the staircase in the small foyer. He was dressed in a beautifully tailored gray open-window suit, white shirt with French cuffs, and an expensive-looking dark blue tie. For a man of seventy plus, he was trim and strikingly good looking. He looked not a day over sixty. This was a man who knew how to project power and intimidation.

"Welcome, Mr. Steelgrave, please let us talk in the library. Perhaps a coffee?"

"Yes, thank you."

He gave a nod to Gino, who was off to fetch the coffee. I followed Signor Moretti through the living-room and into the library; I was as impressed as I was the first time. It was a medium-sized room with a large Persian rug in the center covering a wood parquet floor. There was a small settee, a couple of chairs and a round table in the middle of the rug; all the furniture was Italian baroque. The back wall was a large bookcase filled with several hundred books all first editions and signed. This impressed me most the first time here: that he was so well-read. We entered the library, and he walked over to a small table and picked up something. Turning, he said, "If you wouldn't mind indulging an old man."

He handed me a copy of my second book, *A Life Separate: Together* to sign. Was I summoned because he was upset at how he was portrayed in the book? Then he said,

"I thought you were very fair with how you portrayed our first two meetings in the book. Thank you for fictionalizing them enough that people aren't sure it was this family and me." I signed the book and set it on the table.

Gino walked in with the coffee on a tray and set it down on the table with the book. I walked over and picked up an espresso and sat down in a chair. After taking a sip of my coffee, I began, "Mr. Moretti, you didn't summons me here to sign a book. Why am I here?"

Mr. Moretti smiled, and with a slight tilt of the head and raising of one shoulder, he answered, "That's what I like about you, Mr. Steelgrave, always directly to the point. I need you to do me a favor. My brother's son . . . my nephew, Mauro, is missing. I have been told he has been picked up by the FBI. I know you have some kind of connection with them because of your and my last association. I obviously cannot call the FBI and ask if they have him.

My nephew has never been associated with the family business. He is a computer nerd and works as an independent IT contractor for big companies. Because of his last name, some people and groups cause him trouble to get to me. It has been two weeks he has been missing, and all I hear is the rumor he is in FBI custody. The family is very worried. I'm asking you to use your contacts with the FBI to find out if they have him, and if they do, why."

I sat sipping my coffee, weighing my options. I don't need Signor Moretti as an enemy, and he would owe me a favor; on the other hand, I could find myself involved in something over my head. I finished my coffee, stood, and walked over and put the empty cup back on the tray still thinking. I turned to him and said, "I will make a call, Mr. Moretti, because it is your nephew and a family member, not part of your organization. Don't assume that means I will do anything more in the future. I still feel bad about the death of your son; this makes us even."

With a nod of agreement, he extended his hand, and we shook. We said goodbye, and I left.

He could have called and asked, but I am glad he didn't I wouldn't want someone someday checking his phone records and see we had been talking. Hell, I bet his phones are monitored, and he knows it. That's why I was summoned with a note.

Chapter 6

ON THE DRIVE home, I wondered, where was Jim Dempsey these days and how I would run him down. Jim is with the FBI. He headed up the team that was chasing me around Italy, trying to get the Tesla files I had. He was also responsible for saving my life at my daughter's wedding. He was the contact Signor Moretti knows I have in the FBI.

I arrived home just after 1:30 p.m. I entered the house and headed for the bar to make a martini. I hesitated a moment and decided against it. I think I will stop drinking martinis until after the baptism. The drinking was a little out of hand, and last weekend was proof. I have never embarrassed myself before. I grabbed a cigar from the humidor, then walked to the kitchen, grabbed some left-over chicken out of the fridge, and poured myself an ice-tea. I walked out to the terrace, sat down, put on some jazz, and started to think while I ate my lunch.

Then it came to me. I still had Jim's cell phone number. I grabbed my phone, and after a search I found it. I looked at my watch, 10:30 p.m. on the east coast and 7:30 p.m. on the west coast, not too late to call.

"Hello?"

"Jim, it's Warren Steelgrave."

"How are you, Warren? What a coincidence; your name came up today in a conversation."

"Really? In what context?"

"Nothing important. What's up?"

"Jim, I need a favor."

Jim didn't answer; he just remained silent. I could feel his concentration focus while he is waiting for me to ask the favor.

"What do you know about a Mauro Moretti?"

There was a long silence. Then Jim said, "Are you in Muriaglio?"

Now my concentration focused.

"Yes."

"I am in Turin, let me drive up and meet you for dinner."

"I thought I was calling you in the states. Why are you in Italy?"

"I'll explain at dinner, where shall we meet? Somewhere away from the village."

"Jim, do you know the Tre Re in Castellamonte?"

"I do, Warren."

"Meet you there at 7:30 this evening."

"See you at 7:30 Warren."

I hung up and took a long drag on my cigar and leaned back in the chair to think. "What had I gotten myself into?" It was clear Jim didn't want the conversation to go any further on the phone. I took another long drag and deep in thought reached for my martini and realized it was iced tea. Shit! Maybe this isn't the time to stop drinking.

I got to the Tre Re just before 7:30, and as I walked in, Luciano saw me and came across the lobby to greet me. Luciano, a man in his seventies, was the classic older Italian. Gray hair, trim, and always well dressed, with the movements and manners of an older Fred Astaire.

"Warren, it's good to see you. You haven't been in for quite a while."

"I have been busy finishing a book."

"Your friend is already here, Warren." With a raised eyebrow and an inquisitive look, he went on. "He asked that I seat you both in the back. A beginning of a new book?"

"Maybe, Luciano . . . maybe."

Luciano led me through the restaurant to a small table in the back of the restaurant and away from everyone. I sat down across from Jim, and said, "Mauro Moretti must have been the magic word. What's with all the intrigue?"

"Warren, why were you calling me about Mauro Moretti?"

"I was asked to check and see if he had been picked up by the FBI."

"Who asked, Warren?"

"Jim, it's your turn. We exchange information. It's your turn to answer."

Jim thought for a long time. He didn't want to answer but needed information from me about my source and why they wanted to know. Finally, Jim answered,

"We might have." Jim seeing this answer was getting me very irritated, raised a hand up slightly off the table stopping my response, then continued, "Warren, you know I can't give you any information on an ongoing investigation. *DON'T GET INVOLVED* with this."

"I wouldn't be here, Jim, if I wasn't already involved. I am trying to find out just how involved I am! Why would he be picked up; my understanding is, he has nothing to do with the family business, that he was a computer nerd working freelance for a couple of large companies."

"Warren, I guess you have the answer."

I sat there, puzzled, thinking, "I hated riddles." Then I looked straight at Jim, to read his tell and asked, "Is he dead?"

Jim gave up nothing in a tell; he was prepared for the question. Jim was a great interrogator; he led me to the question he knew I would ask and had his answer ready.

"Warren, I won't answer that. If I say no and he turns up dead, you will think I lied to you. I think you know that the fact I'm here in Italy means he is involved in something major. You will have to trust me; it's in your best interests you don't know. Tell me why you called and asked about Mauro Moretti?"

"His uncle summoned me to his house. The family is worried about him missing. The only information is a rumor the FBI has him. They know we have an association and asked I call and find out."

"I wish I could help you out, Warren, I can't confirm or deny the rumor."

I knew I wasn't going to get any more out of Jim, so I let the questions go. We had a good dinner as always at the Tre Re.

I got home and entering the house I looked over at the bar. Then thought to hell with it, now is not the time to change my routine. I walked to the kitchen and took the gin out of the freezer, walked over to the bar, and made a very cold martini. Grabbing a cigar and the martini, I went out to the terrace to put on some jazz and think. "How does this happen? Mauro Moretti was involved in something over his head. My guess is he hacked into a national database. The FBI wants the world to believe he is alive so that whoever he is working for is smoked out of hiding. Signor Moretti thinks he is alive and wants to retrieve him and punish all involved. Last week, I was looking forward to a relaxing weekend with Maria keeping a long overdue promise. Now I find myself between two powerful organizations with two powerful and smart men using me as bait to smoke out a third group all involved in something; I have no idea what it's about. I have an ex-wife, a lover, and the love of my life coming to spend a weekend. I need another martini."

Chapter 7

THE NEXT MORNING, I called Signor Moretti.

"Pronto."

"Gino, it's Warren Steelgrave; is Signor Moretti available?"

"One minute, please."

After a few moments, I heard Signor Moretti's voice.

"Mr. Steelgrave, how may I help you?"

"I have located some information on a rare book you said you were interested in. If you have time, I will be in Milano this morning. I thought we could meet, and I could give you the information."

Signor, Moretti, responded, "Perhaps lunch?"

"Do you know the Ristorante Galleria, next to Prada in the Galleria?"

"What time?"

"12:30?"

"Good." Then he hung up.

I sat for a moment finishing my coffee, then got up to get ready to leave. I could tell Signor Moretti was irritated that I wouldn't drive all the way to Cremona, but I wanted to make a point; I didn't work for him or was a subject of the king. If he wanted the information, he would have to come to me on neutral ground.

I arrived at the restaurant at about 12:20 p.m. The restaurant is next to Prada in the Galleria. The Galleria is a huge type of mall and simulates a covered city with streets paved in mosaic tiles and a glass ceiling.

The Ristorante Galleria has part of the restaurant extend out on the street, simulating a sidewalk Café. I walked up and introduced myself to the maître d'.

"Buongiorno, I would like a table for three." I figured Gino would be tagging along.

"Mr. Steelgrave?"

"Yes"

"Your party is already here, please follow me."

Following him, we went into and through the main part of the restaurant to a small private room in the back. Entering the room, I saw Gino sitting near the door dressed as always in an impeccable dark suit. In the center of the well-appointed room was a dining room table for six with place settings for two. Signor Moretti was sitting at the head of the table, checking emails on his phone, with a place setting to his left. My place to sit.

I sat down, and a waiter appeared from nowhere and asked for our drink orders. Signore Moretti ordered a glass of red wine, and I ordered a bourbon old fashioned.

"Shall we order first, Mr. Steelgrave?"

I nodded yes as I was looking over the menu. In just a few minutes, the waiter was back with our drinks to take our order. We both ordered the Risotto, and as soon as the waiter left, Signore Moretti asked, "Mr. Steelgrave, what have you found out about my nephew?"

I sat there, taking a sip of my drink, thinking of the rehearsed words I had prepared.

"I met with my contact, and we had a long talk around the subject. He would not confirm if they had him but hinted they do. I asked point-blank if he was dead." This shocked Signore Moretti; this was something he had not considered. I paused a few seconds, then continued, "He wouldn't answer. He said, if he told me he was alive and later your nephew turned up dead, I would accuse him of lying to me."

"What do you think, Mr. Steelgrave, alive or dead?"

"That question puts me in the same spot I was putting my contact in."

I could tell Signor Moretti was beginning to get upset. He set his glass of wine down. He turned to me, having to move his chair slightly so that he was square to me. His eyes were dark and piercing. Looking me straight in the eyes, he said, "Mr. Steelgrave, in our brief encounters, I have come to know you well enough to respect your intuition, gut feelings, and ability to read tells and put them all together to come up with an accurate sense of the situation. Give me your assessment!"

"I think he is dead; the FBI wants everyone to think he is alive. I think your nephew knowingly or not, got mixed up with a group that used him to hack a National Security or Defense Data Base. I think this group then thought they had killed him, leaving him for dead, but the FBI picked him up, and he died in their custody, or maybe he was dead. They want the world to think he is alive and recovering, so the group that left him for dead will come out of hiding. You can see the position you and my contact put me in. I am the bait. They will come for me thinking I know the answer."

"What will you do, Mr. Steelgrave?"

"I don't have much choice, do I? I will have to play, hide and seek until the FBI captures them or you kill them."

Just then, our lunch came. All through lunch, nothing more was said. After eating, I excused myself and rose from my seat to leave. Signor Moretti rising from his seat, extended his hand to shake mine. Shaking my hand, he said, "Thank you, Mr. Steelgrave, be safe."

I nodded and left. I could tell all through lunch Signore Moretti was deep in thought. He never considered that his nephew was dead or that he had gotten involved way over his head with a group. Instead of his nephew being picked up by the FBI over some drug charge or something similar, this new group could pose a threat to his family and business. He was very concerned.

As I walked through the Galleria, I had a sense I was being followed. I headed to the entrance that opened onto the Piazza del Duomo, where the crowd would be larger and easier for me to lose a tail. The Duomo di Milano was across the piazza to my left. It was stunning, gleaming white in the bright spring sunlight against a dark blue cloudless sky.

The crowd was large, and to play it safe, I bought a ticket to tour the inside. I entered the Duomo, which is the fifth-largest in the world and can hold forty thousand people. I got into the center of a large tour group and walked along with them until they passed a large column. I slipped out of the crowd and stood behind the column, which gave me a large view of the interior. After about ten minutes, sure enough, I saw two men walking through, one on each side of the Duomo searching for someone: me.

They passed by me, and I got in amongst a group heading the opposite way toward the exit. Leaving the Duomo, I headed straight to the hotel where I parked the car. I wasn't going to be followed into a parking garage, so I pulled into the entrance of a large hotel and had the valet park the car telling them I was meeting someone for lunch.

Having retrieved my car, I headed home. "Who was following me? They weren't dressed well enough to be FBI. Were they Moretti's men keeping an eye on me or some still unknown group?"

Chapter 8

I ARRIVED AT MY home in Muriaglio a little before 6:00 p.m. I could relax here. The village is so small, only about two hundred people; any strangers in town would be noticed at once. It was too early for dinner, so I decided to work on a poem I had started. I poured myself an iced tea, grabbed a cigar and a lightweight jacket, and went out to the terrace to write. It was almost night, just a ribbon of red on the horizon just above the roofs of the village. It was calm with a chill in the air.

Being told Cindy was coming to the baptism threw me for a loop. It stirred a lot of suppressed emotions. Putting them on paper in the form of a poem was my way of dealing with them. I struggled with finding the right words to add to the poem for about an hour before putting it away. I was getting hungry and decided to walk up the street and have dinner at *La Terrazza Sul Canavese*.

I walked out and started down the stairs of my house. As I got to the bottom and started to the front gate, I saw the shadowy figure in the small alleyway between my house and my neighbors. I rushed to the gate and looked up the small alley, but it was gone. I turned and went back upstairs and checked the front door to make sure it was locked, then went on to dinner.

The next morning, I was having my morning coffee and thinking over the events of the day before. I really did not want to bring a lot of drama to the village. I decided I would go to Florence for a while. I love the city and have been wanting to pick up a new set of hand-painted dishes for the house. I got on the internet and rented a small apartment a few blocks from the church of *Santa Croce*.

Now to call Maria and to let her know I will be in Florence. I must give her an excuse as to why I am not staying with her. This will not be easy.

"Pronto."

"Ciao, Maria. It's Warren."

"Ciao, Warren, it's good to hear your voice. What's up?"

"I am coming to Florence for about two weeks on a little business and wanted to let you know."

"Great, you can stay here. I won't be here. My dad is getting worse, and I am taking him to Paris for tests and will be gone most of that time."

"I will be very busy and will rent an apartment. I would feel uncomfortable staying at your place without you."

"Are you sure, Warren?"

"I am sure. You take care of your father, and we will find some time to be together."

"When do you arrive in Florence?"

"Friday."

"We leave for Paris on Sunday. Call when you get here, and we can do something on Friday."

"Sounds like a plan, Maria, See you Friday."

Easier than I thought. The rest of the week was quiet. Nothing unusual; no strangers nothing. It led me to believe, somehow, they know I am leaving for Florence.

On Friday I had my cousin Gino take me to the train station in Turin. I arrived in Florence just before noon and took a taxi to meet the property manager on Via Delle Pinzochare. After signing the lease agreement, I walked to the restaurant Cucina Torcicoda on Via Torta for something to eat. I ordered lunch, and while waiting for it to be served, I called Maria.

"Pronto"

"Ciao Maria I am here in Florence."

"Great, Warren. I have a little more to do, I can meet you around 3:00 this afternoon; is that OK."

"Perfect. I will meet you at the Café Dumo at 3:00.

I sat eating my lunch memorizing faces of all who came in alone and what they were wearing. I finished my lunch and headed over to a little ceramic shop near the Palazzo Vecchio to order my hand-painted dishes. I walked with the crowds on the main streets, avoiding any pass-throughs and alleys.

After ordering the dishes, I made my way over to Café Duomo and entered. The Café Duomo is located across the street from the Cattedrale di Maria del Fiore. It was here that I fell in love with Cindy O'Brian. We would have coffee here every day after class.

Mauro saw me right away and greeted me with a large smile. He walked up to me, giving me a large hug and said in a loud excited voice, "Signor Steelgrave, my old

friend, how have you been?" Then standing back a step and looking at me before I could answer, he continued. "I heard about Cindy and the serial killer. I am glad she was OK. How is she doing?"

I smiled and said, "I have been fine, and Cindy is living in America and doing well."

"Good to hear. Follow me, I will sit you at your old table. By yourself?"

"No. I will be meeting a woman shortly."

Walking through the café, I saw him. One of the men that went into the restaurant; sitting drinking a coffee. How did he know to be here?

"What can I get you, Warren?"

"I will wait until she gets here, Mauro."

They must be monitoring either mine or Maria's phone. I just saw on the news that Google listens to all conversations near phones. You don't even have to be on a call.

I see Mauro leading Maria through the café, and I stand to greet her. I pull out her chair, and as she is sitting, Mauro, who is standing behind her, looks at me with a smile and quickly raises both eyebrows twice.

"What would you like, Maria?"

Turning to Mauro, she says, "An espresso, please."

"I'll have a double espresso and a torta, Mauro."

I sat there wondering how much I should tell her about my situation when she said,

"Warren, I am going to the bathroom to wash up."

"Good idea, I will go with you. I need to wash my hands."

Before she could get up, I reached for her hand. When she looked at me, I gave her a stern look and, with a subtle move, placed my napkin over my phone. Looking confused, she did the same. We went down the small hallway, and before going into the men's room, I said, "Our conversations are being monitored through our phones. I will explain later."

Chapter 9

WE CAME OUT of the bathroom just as our coffees were being placed on our table. I looked over at the gentleman who was following me; he was gone. Replaced by someone new no doubt; an old trick in tailing a person. A proper tail always involves several men.

We finished our coffee, and Maria asked what I would like to do until dinner.

"I would like to walk over to the Bargello Museum and see the bronze David by Donatello. If it weren't for Cosimo de Medici commissioning this statue, art would have remained in the dark ages. So different from the David by Michelangelo. This nude young boy, with his hand on his hip. It is one of my favorites in all of Florence."

"Good, Warren, let's go."

We got up and left.

"Maria, did you drive?"

"No. I walked; it's not far from my office."

We took our time walking to the Bargello. I love walking the streets of Florence, thinking of all the greats that

walked these same streets: Cimabue, Gaddo, Gaddi, Giotto, and Brunelleschi, just to name a few.

After touring the museum, Maria asked where I would like to have dinner. I suggested the Golden View near the Ponte Vecchio. She smiled.

"That is one of my favorites," she replied, and we were off to the restaurant. As we entered the Golden View, I said to the hostess, "The lady would like to check her purse."

"Certainly."

As the hostess reached for Maria's purse, Maria looked at me with a concerned look. I raised my eyebrows and smiled as I dropped my phone in it. Without taking her eyes off me with a stern look, she handed over the purse.

"If you would follow me, I will show you to your table."

We walked behind the hostess, and I leaned close to Maria and said, "Sorry, Maria, I know how women hate to be separated from their purses, but it's important. I will explain at dinner."

We ordered drinks and our meals. When the waiter left with our order, I looked around and quietly said, "I have myself in a little bit of trouble and have picked up a tail. That's why I came to Florence. That's why I don't want to stay at your place or in the village until I get this cleared up. I don't want to involve you in this. I don't think it will take very long. I should be done with it by the time you get back from Paris.

I think they are listening to our conversations on one or both of our phones. After I told you the other night I was coming, they were here waiting for me. After settling in at my rented apartment, I went to lunch. I paid close attention to everyone who came in. After I called you and we agreed to meet at Café Duomo. When I got there, one of the men who came into the restaurant was already there, drinking coffee."

I watched her facial expression go from curious to worry to something between anger and disappointment. Shaking her head slightly and pursing her lips a little, she said, "Warren, what am I to do with you? Every time I see you, it's something different, and yet it is always the same."

"I am sorry, Maria. It's not like I go looking for it. It's been this way my whole life."

I went on to explain the whole thing, starting with the encounter outside her apartment with Signore Moretti's man Piero.

"Warren, this sounds serious. Moretti is no one to get involved with."

"I am not worried about him. In fact, it might be his men tailing me. He has a vested interest in protecting me, as does the FBI. They both are using me as bait to find a third party. It does them no good if I should disappear. I think the third group, whomever they are, just want to find out what I learned from the FBI. That's why I think it will be over quickly. After about three days, I will be no good to any of them."

"Still, Warren, I think . . ."

I raised a hand and stopped her from continuing.

"Maria, please let's change the subject. I have something else I need to tell you about the baptism. I have given you the date, but feel I should let you know Stephanie has asked Cindy to be the Godmother."

I looked at Maria, waiting for a reaction. She just sat there a moment or two thinking, then said, "Warren, let me get this straight. I will be there with you and your ex-lover, who will be the Godmother and your second wife."

It all sounded even worse, hearing her say it. Then she smiled and continued in a slow, methodical voice,

"I think it will be a very interesting weekend. Shall we go back to my place?"

"I will get a taxi and drop you off. I don't think I should stay."

"Warren, can you answer something for me?"

"Sure, Maria, anything."

"Why do I have the feeling you feel guilty about having slept with me? Ever since that weekend, you have been distant like you have cheated on Cindy. A woman who is sleeping every night with her husband. A woman who left you and you haven't talked to in eighteen months."

I sat there quiet for a while, trying to find the right words so as not to hurt her.

I thought, "You're right, I do feel like I cheated. I can't explain it any more than a friend I asked the same question of. He had been married twenty years when his wife left him. It had been ten years, and he still wore his wedding ring and never dated. I tell you this because I have too much respect for you to not be honest. I tell myself repeatedly the same thing I told him. This is stupid; move on with your life." But I answered her, "It's not like that. It's the family coming and being followed that has me upset. I am concerned about getting you all caught up in my life's drama."

What I can tell you is, I am working on it. That is why I am here. Our last weekend was wonderful, minus the Absinthe. I was looking forward to being here with you. But things have gotten complicated. I hope you can be a little patient with me."

"I do understand, Warren. I have waited this long. I can be very patient. Shall we go?"

We stood and headed out of the restaurant, and as I was paying, I saw a man drinking all by himself at the end of the bar. Maria retrieved her purse, and we walked out. I took Maria by the arm, and we hurried to the right and at the corner turned right onto the crowded Ponte Vecchio and went into a shop selling gold.

"*Buonasera*, may I show you something?"

"Just looking," I replied. I never took my eyes off the street. A few moments later, the man sitting at the bar came hurriedly by, with his focus down the street. I took Maria by the arm and leaving the shop, turned left the way we had come. At the corner, we turned left onto the street with the Golden View restaurant. A taxi was just letting out his passengers at the restaurant. I put Maria into the taxi and gave her a kiss. I could see the concern in her eyes.

"I will be all right, Maria. I will call you in the morning. I need to follow that guy when he comes back this way. I shut the taxi door and leaned in the driver's opened window. Giving the driver a one hundred euro note, I said, "Take a long way home to make sure her husband isn't following."

The driver broke out with a big smile and gave a wink and a nod. He drove off, and I stepped back into a small dark alley to wait.

Chapter 10

"Hello"

"Aashiq. It's Dabir. I lost Steelgrave and the woman in the crowds after they left the restaurant. I am on my way to meet Erol and wait for Steelgrave at his apartment."

"It's important to get what information he has within a day or two. Don't screw this up as you did with Mauro Moretti."

"I swear he was dead when we left him."

"And the protocol he had developed, Dabir? Where is it? The rumor is, the FBI has Mauro, and he is recovering. If he does, he can tell them where he had hidden it. We must get to it before the FBI. You should have found out where Mauro hid it before you attempted to kill him."

"We thought we had beaten that information out of him. Before we could verify it, the FBI showed up, and we had to kill him. We did kill him!"

"Maybe you did. Maybe you didn't. Maybe Steelgrave knows. We must find out Steelgrave's involvement before we put the plan in motion."

"We will pick him up, and whatever information he has, he will give up it before we kill him."

***

I waited in that damp, smelly alley nearly forty-five minutes before I decided the man tailing me wasn't coming back this way. I stepped out and got a taxi and headed for one of Maria's apartments. I got to the apartment and went in.

Maria had given me a key at dinner to a vacant studio apartment on Via Roma near the church Saint Maria Novella. We both anticipated the apartment I rented was being watched, and it best I not go back there tonight.

I laid on the bed listening to jazz on my phone to relax. Then Johnny Harman started singing the song, *I Could Write A Book*. My mind drifted off to the first time I met Cindy. She was late on the first day of class. I was busy finishing my homework and didn't notice her walk-in; until the chair next to me pulled out, and she said, "May I sit here?"

I was twenty-four years older than her and madly in love. For three years, we were apart, and that love sustained me without a problem. This time she has been gone for eighteen months, and it is difficult. Maria is right. It's time to let it go and start my life again. I have been living alone, drinking, and writing. I feel so guilty about being with Maria. Why I ask myself why do I feel like I am cheating on Cindy every time I am with Maria. This has got to stop; Cindy is home with her family, and it is time for me to explore a future with Maria.

***

"Hello?"

"Dabir? It's Aashiq. Where are you."

"We are watching Steelgrave's apartment near Piazza San Croce."

"I had his phone tracked. It's near the Piazzale Michelangelo. What shall we do?"

Aashiq thought for a moment then replied, "Stay in place; he has to come back sooner or later. He is probably staying with the girl tonight and will return in the morning. I will try and find out who she is."

***

I got up early the next morning, showered, and got dressed. There was no food in the apartment, and I was dying for a cup of coffee. I had to retrieve my backpack from the rented apartment. I wondered how I was going to do that as I left. I knew the rented apartment was being watched.

It was a bright morning; the air smelled so fresh from the early morning thunderstorm. I love this time of day in Florence. Everyone on the streets walking with a purpose to get somewhere for work or school. All of the tourists haven't gotten up yet. In another hour, there would be an entirely different crowd on the streets.

As I got to within two blocks of the apartment, my senses started to focus. I turned the corner, and as I looked down the street, I saw a sedan parked near the apartment with two men. Had to be FBI; no one else would be that conspicuous. My first thought was good. I would be able to get into the apartment without being abducted.

As I got closer to the car, they got out. It was Jim Dempsey and a friend. I walked up to Jim and said, "Buongiorno Jim, please come in; let's not talk on the street."

I unlocked the wooden front door to the building and went in with Jim and his friend following behind. My apartment was the first one on the left, just inside the door to the building. I unlocked it, and we all went into the apartment. I shut the door and turned to the two men. Jim said, "Warren, let me introduce you to special agent John Ramsey."

I reached and shook his hand. Jim was looking around the apartment and saw my backpack on the couch and the lease agreement on the kitchen table.

"Gee, Warren, still haven't unpacked?"

"No, I just got here yesterday; dropped off my stuff and left to meet a friend. I picked up a tail along the way, lost them, and didn't come back until now."

Special agent Ramsey walked over to the window, and standing behind the curtains started watching the street. I started walking to the small kitchen.

"Shall we have a seat, Jim. I wish I had something to offer you."

"That's OK, Warren, we won't be very long. I wanted to ask you a few questions about your meeting with Signor Moretti last Tuesday."

"There is not much to say. We met, I told Signor Moretti I had met with you and asked if you had his son. I told him you wouldn't confirm or deny it, which leads me to believe you do. I think it was what he wanted to believe. He seemed relieved."

Jim sat there thinking for a minute, then said, "Did he mention anything about codes?"

"No, Jim, he didn't! Are you going to tell me what this is all about?"

Jim sat there rubbing his finger around on the tabletop thinking.

"Warren, the FBI needs your help on this. Mauro Moretti was hired by an international firm to help with their computer security. The company does a lot of work designing weapon systems for the defense department. They were being hit daily by hackers. One got through, but only to some minor files. Mauro was hired to look at the system and see where they might be vulnerable. He started by attacking the system. If he got in, he would make a change to plug it. In doing so repeatedly, he realized he had developed a protocol for hacking any system. My understanding is that it's about three pages. Realizing what he had done, he was on his way to deliver it to us when he was abducted and tortured and left dying.

The FBI arrived, forcing the abductors to flee. He died before he could give us any information, other than that it was hidden, and the abductors didn't get it.

Warren, do you know if Signor Moretti knows of the protocol? It would be worth a lot of money on the black market. What we would like you to do is find out what information you can from Signor Moretti. If he knows of it or where it could be hidden, etcetera."

I answered, being both surprised and irritated. "You want me to interrogate Signor Moretti? What am I supposed to do, ask to see him, and then beat the information from him? You make no sense sometimes. He would never give me any information, especially if he wants the protocol."

"Hear me out, Warren. I have some information you and Signor Moretti need to have to truly understand the situation you both are in. I think he will see why he needs to help you find the protocol."

Chapter 11

GREAT, I THOUGHT. I WAS planning to hide out until everyone involved realized Mauro was dead, and I wasn't involved in any of this. Instead, I'm being asked to go on a treasure hunt that could cost me my life. I sat there, just staring at him and nodded for him to go on.

"Warren, you need to explain to Signor Moretti his whole family is in danger as is yours. I wasn't at liberty to give you this information the other night at dinner. After discussions within the bureau, I convinced them we need your help. I had to convince them I believed you would not let Signor Moretti get and sell the protocol. We need his help with all the contacts he has on the street to develop leads. Information from family members about Mauro's closet friends. We need your help convincing him to help. The FBI will furnish what technical support and other resources needed."

I sat there thinking, "I don't really have a choice with family coming in just a few weeks."

"Jim, I will need an encrypted phone to start."

Jim set one on top of a file he had set on the table.

"This phone is an encrypted satellite phone." Then he set another one on the table. "This one is for Moretti. Read through the file before meeting with Moretti. This group is the most vicious we have ever come across. They call themselves *Allah's Army* and are a very small group, only about twenty-five persons. Their leader is a man called Aashiq and is a very rich man; he funds the group. What makes them so dangerous is that the group is small. No internet traffic, or courier's explosives, etc. They are very hard to keep tabs on. Aashiq is not about lots of actions killing people and causing widespread fear. He is about taking down the whole electrical grid or banking system of a country from a small hidden villa."

I sat there thinking through what Jim was telling me and what he was leaving out. "Sure, the protocol was important to find, but finding Aashiq and killing him was just as important." The group is small; this was also their weakness. Unlike the large terrorist groups, if you captured the leader, there was no one to take his place. The FBI wanted this guy before his way of thinking caught on.

"Count me in, Jim, as if I have a choice. I feel like a worm at the end of a fishing line being cast into a lake."

Jim smiled and stood, pushing his chair back to the table.

"Be careful, Warren, this Aashiq will stop at nothing. He is sadistic and enjoys torturing people. Women and children, it doesn't matter if it gets him what he wants. Do you have a gun?"

"No."

"I'll get you one."

"No, Jim, don't do that. I'm not sure I would know how to use it. I'll be OK."

I stood with him, and we walked to the front door. Special agent Ramsey followed. We shook hands, and they left. I turned and walked over to my backpack and took out my old untraceable phone; I called Maria.

"Pronto."

"Ciao, Maria, it's Warren."

"I was beginning to worry, Warren. I still have your phone; how are you calling me?"

"I'll explain when I see you. What would you like to do today?"

"Anything, Warren. I just want to spend time with you."

"I would like to have another picnic near the Arno."

"Perfect, Warren. I have things here to prepare lunch."

"I'll bring the wine. See you in about an hour."

I hung up the phone. After a shower and change of clothes, I packed my backpack as a go-bag. I walked over and looked out the window from behind the curtains. I could see no one; in fact, the street was empty. Just then, a small party of tourists appeared on the street, walking the direction of the taxi stand at the end of the street. Quickly I left the apartment and started walking with the group. At the end of the street, I got into a taxi and told him to drop me at the Piazza del Duomo. I knew this part of town was restricted to cars; only taxis and buses were allowed.

"Can you tell if we are being followed?"

"Si, signore."

"Good. If we are, I will give you an extra fifty euros if you lose them."

I could see him looking at me in the rear-view mirror: He smiled. He took a long way, and when he dropped me, he said we were followed, but he left them in traffic. I thanked him and paid the extra fifty.

I walked past the Cattedrale di Santa Maria del Fiore and into the Café Duomo.

"Ciao Warren!"

"Ciao Mauro, a double espresso, please."

I walked to my favorite table and sat down. Mauro brought my coffee and set it down on the table.

"Mauro, I need you to do something for me."

"Sure, Warren."

"I need you to get a message to Signor Moretti. I want to come to his house tomorrow. If it's OK, I need him to give me a time. Text me at this number. If OK, text just the time, if not just text no."

Mauro took the slip of paper and put it in the pocket on his apron. With a concerned look, he nodded and walked away back to the counter. I sat there drinking my coffee, waiting to see if anyone would come in. No one did. I finished my coffee and started to Maria's apartment.

Chapter 12

"HELLO?"

"Dabir, it's Aashiq. Have you found Steelgrave?"

"Yes, it was as you said he came back to the apartment this morning. Two men were waiting for him in a car with U.S. government license plates; FBI, I guess. They stayed awhile then left; a little later, Steelgrave left. He took a taxi, and we followed but lost him in traffic. Then we went to the location of his phone to wait."

Aashiq was thinking. "Why was the FBI there?" Then the thought came to him. "The FBI must not know where the protocol is and think Steelgrave might know."

"Dabir, do not pick him up. Just follow him until I figure out what his part is in all of this."

***

I left the café Duomo with a bottle of wine and got into a taxi and headed for Maria's apartment. I arrived at Maria's close to 10:30 a.m. and rang her apartment. I heard the door unlock and went in and up the stairs to her apartment. She was standing in the doorway, wearing only a robe.

"Good morning, Maria."

"Buongiorno, Warren. Come in, I am almost ready. A coffee?"

"No, thank you. I have had plenty already this morning."

I walked in and shut the door behind me. I turned, and Maria put her arms around me. Pulling me close, she kissed me and said, "Make love to me before we go."

I kissed her back and felt her undo my belt. Her hair was freshly washed, and the light scent of the shampoo mixed with her natural scent was driving me wild. I barely got undressed when we were on the floor. She took the lead, and we made love in every way imaginable. After we took a shower together, washing each other. When we were dressing, Maria said to me, "Warren, are you all right?"

I looked at my arms and knees for bruises from the tile floor and replied, "Not too bad I have had worse, and they weren't as fun to receive, and you?"

She hit me in the arm. "I mean, were you followed last night?"

"I was, but I lost them. The FBI was at my apartment this morning when I arrived. I'm sure I was followed here. I am glad you are leaving for a while. I should have this all behind me by the time you return. They gave me a satellite phone that can't be traced. Write down this number in case you must reach me. I wouldn't use your current phone; pick up another prepaid phone."

"Warren, this sounds serious."

I raise a shoulder nodding my head and raising both eyebrows.

"Maybe, not sure yet. I do know I don't want you involved."

I pulled her close and gave her a long kiss. Then said, "Don't worry, I am sure it will be over in a short time; two weeks at the longest . . . I want to forget about it for today. I just want to enjoy your company."

We finished dressing, and on the way out, Maria picked up the bottle of wine I had brought off the floor and put it into the picnic basket she had prepared. We left through the front door, and Maria locked it. We were off. Outside the apartment building, I asked her where we were going.

"I am taking you to my favorite park, Warren."

It was a beautiful day. It was going to warm up today, not hot, but one of those warm spring days that still would have a coolness to the light breeze as it crossed over your skin. It had rained last night, and the air smelled so clean. We walked along, holding hands, and all was right in the world.

After about twenty minutes, we arrived at a small hidden park on a secluded residential street. The park was maybe two acres on the side of a hill with lots of grass and trees. We walked through the park until we found an area of lawn shaded by a large tree; it looked out across the Arno and the city of Florence. We spread out a blanket to sit on, and Maria started taking our lunch out of the basket. As I was opening the wine, she said to me, "Warren, I want to know all about you. I want you to tell me everything. I want you to tell me about each of your wives and children."

I poured us each a glass of wine and sat down on the blanket next to her. I started first asking her about her family; her dad and his age, her mom and brothers, and sisters. Then it was my turn. She wanted to know most about my children and my relationship with them. It was difficult for her to understand why I would live in Italy and be away from them and the grandchildren. It felt like I was interviewing for the position of husband. It was becoming clear to me if I wasn't going to commit to marriage and another family, this was going to be a short-lived love affair. The rest of the afternoon was spent in intimate conversations about our childhood and families. It was so different from being with Cindy. We would talk about art and our dreams for the future. The afternoon was becoming late, and it was getting a little chilly; it was time to go.

Walking back to her apartment, I asked, "Shall we go to dinner tonight?"

"I am sorry, Warren, I have to pack and go to my parent's house. We all leave for Paris very early tomorrow."

I nodded, I understood and kissed her. After she entered the building, I started to my apartment.

Chapter 13

"HELLO?"

"Aashiq, it's Dabir. Steelgrave just dropped the girl off at home. They spent the whole day in a park lying on a blanket having a picnic. I am sure she is not involved."

Aashiq remained quiet thinking, then he said, "Have someone watch her; to see if she goes out. And keep an eye on Steelgrave."

"OK"

***

I decided to walk to my apartment. As the day slowly turned to night, the air was getting very chilly. I took my scarf out of my coat pocket and wrapped it around my neck. I zipped up my coat, turned up the collar, and with my hands deep in my pockets, headed for home. It was only a thirty-minute walk, and I wanted the time to think.

Why was I feeling guilty about spending time with Maria? It was because I did care for her and didn't want to involve her in my life of drama. Then I laughed to myself and thought, don't pretend to be noble; the truth is it's about having more children. It's not guilt you feel it's that you do not want to lose her. It's that you don't want more children. Young children would only tie you down for the rest of your life. It was always hard for me to confront my own selfishness. The argument was always the same; I would doubt my motives, and the debate would start in my head as to why I felt one way or another. Was I selfish or practical? Was I concerned about the other person's well-being or justifying what it was I wanted? Finally, I laughed out loud and said to myself, "Hell, you will probably be dead before she gets back from Paris. It will work itself out in time."

I was just passing a very nice-looking restaurant and decided to go in and have dinner. I wasn't seated for very long when a well-dressed gentleman approached the table, and in a tone that made it clear there would be no debate, said, "Signore, please come with me."

I got up and followed him down a small hallway in the back of the restaurant that led to the bathrooms and back door. Standing with the door open was Signor Moretti's man Piero. He motioned me through the door into a small alley with a car waiting. We got into the back seat, and the car drove off.

"Signor, Moretti wants to have dinner with you."

There was nothing else to be said. I relaxed and leaned back into the soft leather seat.

After about ten minutes, we turned into an alley, and the car stopped behind a restaurant. We got out of the car, and I was led through the backdoor and down a hall to a small banquet room. The room was very elegant with oil paintings on the walls. A crystal chandelier hung from a wood-paneled ceiling over an antique wood dining table; the table had place settings for two. Sitting at the place setting at the head of the table was Signor Moretti holding a glass of red wine.

"Good Evening, Mr. Steelgrave, please have a seat."

I walked over and sat at the place setting to his left.

"I received a message you wanted to meet."

A waiter appeared out of nowhere and poured me a glass of wine, then disappeared.

I picked up my glass of wine and took a sip giving me a moment to settle down and organize my thoughts. Then, I began. I explained my last meeting with the FBI. I went through the details of what was told to me and how the FBI thought we should handle finding the file. I left out their concerns that Signor Moretti would keep the file and sell it. When I had finished, Signor Moretti signaled with his hand to someone behind me and said, "I took the liberty to order dinner for the two of us. I hope that was OK."

I nodded, it was.

Two waiters appeared and served our dinner. Throughout dinner, there was no discussion of my dissertation. I could tell he was using dinner to think through all that I had said. We had a lite conversation about the food, the weather, and the importance of Florence to Western civilization. After dessert and coffee, he ordered two Marcellas. Twirling his wine in his glass, he said, "Explain to me again why I should work with the FBI."

"First, you would be honoring your brother's family by honoring the wishes of his son, your nephew Mauro. He did inform the FBI; was on his way with the protocol because he knew the safety of the world was more important than making money. Second, the FBI has more resources with which to help us."

"Us? Why are you doing this?"

"Do I have a choice? You and the FBI stuck me in the middle of this. You asked me to contact the FBI. After that meeting, I picked up a tail. I'm sure they think the FBI gave me information, and they are deciding when to pick me up to get that information before killing me."

He took the rest of the wine in the glass in one gulp, set the glass down on the table, and said, "What do you want me to do?"

"Your family is the best source of information on Mauro and where he might have hidden the protocol. You need to get me a lead of where he might have hidden them. I will go about my life as if I'm not part of any of this. We have to act quickly; it won't take who is ever after me long to realize that Mauro is dead, and then they will come for me.

Signor Moretti stood and reached out his hand to shake. Shaking hands, he said, "How do you want me to contact you when I have gathered the information?

"I think by messenger. Have someone drop it off at the Café Duomo. Use this phone if you need to contact me. It can't be monitored."

"Stay safe, Steelgrave; I will have you dropped where you want."

I turned to leave, and Piero was standing by the door, waiting to leave. As I got into the car, Piero said, "The driver will take you to where you want."

After making sure we weren't followed, I had him drop me off close to the first restaurant. I walked down the alley behind the restaurant. Next door was another restaurant; I walked in through the back door, through the restaurant, and out the front door and headed for the apartment.

***

"Dabir!" There he is."

Dabir put his phone away; he was just about to call Aashiq and tell him they lost Steelgrave again. It was a call he didn't want to make. He thought dinner was taking longer than it should and sent Erol in to see why.

"Erol, you just came out of the restaurant. You said he was not in there and must have left out the back."

"He wasn't Dabir; he came out next door; we must have made a mistake as to which restaurant he went in."

Dabir was sure he hadn't made a mistake.

Chapter 14

IT WAS A chilly night as I walked down the deserted street to my rented apartment. I pulled up the collar of my jacket above my scarf and zipped it up. I started thinking of all the personal history I have had in this city. The memories are good and bad. This was the city where I started my new life after my wife died. The city where I met Cindy O'Brian. I looked up, and the moon was rising above the Ponte Vecchio; I stopped and stared at it a moment. I wondered if Cindy had looked at the moon tonight and was thinking of me. Just then, my personal cell phone began to vibrate. I took it out of my pocket and looked at the screen. It was Cindy. It's been eighteen months. Why call now?

"Hello?"

"Hello, Warren, how are you?"

I stopped walking and trying to hide my surprise responded.

"I'm fine, and you?"

With a voice that seemed to be filled with remorse, she responded, "You have been on my mind all day. I have been feeling very anguished, are you sure you are not in any danger."

"No, Cindy, I have just finished dinner with a friend, and I'm on my way back to an apartment I have rented in Florence."

"I assume Stephanie has told you I was asked to be the godmother and will be coming to the baptism."

"She did."

"I wasn't sure what to say to her. I have been so conflicted with my feelings about Italy and all the good memories and very bad memories. I said yes, so I could return and resolve some of the conflicts. I hope you understand."

"I do."

"Stay Safe, Warren. Goodnight."

"Goodnight, Cindy, thanks for the call."

I stood there looking at the moon and thinking that we are still connected. She knew I was lying. I could tell she was also lying. Things weren't well at home. She agreed to be godmother as an excuse to come to Muriaglo to see if I was available and if she could deal with the memory of almost being killed there. I guess we will always be connected in a very special way. This baptism is turning out to be a week of total drama. God help me get through it.

I got to my apartment and went in. I started to grab a cigar and realized I did not bring anything to make a martini. I put back the cigar, walked over and put on some jazz, and sat down to think. How was I going to find the protocol?

***

"Hello?"

"Aashiq, it's Dabir. Steelgrave is almost to his apartment. There is no one on the street, shall we pick him up now?"

There was a long pause while Aashiq was thinking. Then he responded, "No. I don't think Steelgrave has any information yet. If the FBI knew where the protocol was, they would just go and get them. We know Steelgrave has met with the Moretti family. If they had the protocol, we would have heard about it being offered for sale. I think the FBI is using Steelgrave and his relationship with signor Moretti to find out where they might be and to retrieve them. Mauro Moretti must be dead. The FBI wants the Moretti family to think he is alive and is using Steelgrave to negotiate his release. Let's just follow Steelgrave. I have researched him. He is very smart, and if anyone can gather information from the Moretti family and find the hiding place, he will.

***

The next morning, I awoke without an answer on how or where to begin my search for the protocol. I concluded Mauro would have saved them on a thumb drive. A thumb would be much easier to hide someplace.

***

I got up, showered, got dressed, and headed out to Café Duomo for a cappuccino and a brioche. I walked in and nodded to Mauro with a glance and headed to a table in the back. He nodded that he understood and began my cappuccino. Mauro set down my cappuccino and brioche with an envelope. Seeing the envelope, I looked with a questioning look. Mauro raised both eyebrows and, with a stern look said, "Be very careful, my friend," and walked away.

I knew it was from Signor Moretti. I opened it, and there was a small handwritten two-page note and a key. "Signor Steelgrave, I have found out my nephew, Mauro, had a secret office in the city of Lucca near his main office. I have provided a key and address to that office; maybe you will find information there that will lead you to the protocol."

I guess this is a start. It is about two hours by train, I will go this morning. I took out my phone and checked out the train times. There was a train leaving in an hour. I finished my coffee and got up to leave. As I was paying on the way-out, Mauro handed me my receipt, and with a concerned look, he said, "I worry for you, Warren. Be careful these are very bad people, that you cannot trust."

"I know." Then I left headed for the Santa Maria Novella train station. I knew I was being followed, and they could tell I was taking the train by the direction I was headed. I was timing myself to arrive at the station just in time for me to buy a ticket at a kiosk. This way, they could not question anyone as to where I was going, nor would they have time to buy a ticket for the same train. They would know I was leaving town, but where or for how long? The train stopped at several cities.

Two trains were leaving within minutes of each other. I got on my train moments before the door closed, and it left the station. I sat back, put in my earbuds, and started listening to some Chet Baker. It was not long before my mind drifted off to Maria and Cindy.

I was startled out of my meditation by the train jerking as it slowed down, coming into the station at Lucca.

Chapter 15

I GOT OFF THE train and headed to an internet café just down the street from the hotel Lucca. I entered the café and ordered an espresso. Connecting to the internet, I searched for the address in the note on a street map of Lucca. The office was located on Via del Peso about one quarter mile away. I finished my coffee and headed to 255 Via del Peso. I blended in with the people on the street and was sure I wasn't being followed. I arrived at the small office building at about 11:35 a.m. The office was on the second floor, but the glass front door to the building was locked. You had to be buzzed in. I waited a few minutes, and I saw someone inside coming down the stairs and crossing the lobby headed for the front door. I walked up to the door with my keys in my hand just as he got to the door. He opened the door on his way out and held it open for me to enter as I put my keys back into my pocket. I said, "Buongiorno. Grazie."

He gave me a nod and a smile and was off in a hurry, probably late for a lunch appointment. I crossed the lobby and headed up the stairs. When I reached the second floor,

I could go left or right down a long hallway: I went left. Good choice the numbers on the office doors were getting larger. I was soon standing in front of 225. I tried the key; it fit. I unlocked the door and went in. I closed the door behind me and stood a moment and surveyed my surroundings.

The office was small without windows. It had a desk against the left wall with only a chair at the desk and another chair against the back wall with a coat rack just inside the door. No photos or pictures, just bare walls, and a beige vinyl-tile floor. A serious workspace and not for receiving guests. The desk was an old antique carved door set on top of two, two drawer file cabinets and covered with a large clear piece of glass. Very classy. Very original, I thought. Mauro was obviously a creative thinker and would be very creative in a hiding place.

I walked over to the desk and sat down. I started my search with the obvious places; first, the file cabinet on the left. I took out all the files and checked to see if something might be lying on the bottom of the cabinet. There wasn't. Then I started going through the files one at a time, replacing them back in the cabinet as I finished my search. Then I did the same with the other file cabinet. There was nothing of interest. I sat there thinking, "What had he used this office for?" There were only about ten files in each file cabinet. The main use of the file cabinets was to support the desktop. No computer: he must have used a laptop. Why the small secret office? Most of his work had to be done at his main office, and I know the FBI has been all through that. I sat there, then it came to me. In a detective story I had read, the main character had hidden some evidence under the center drawer of this desk.

I next stood up and turned the chair over, nothing. I laid down on the floor and looked under the desk, not covered by the filing cabinets: nothing. Next, I pulled out all the files in the left, top filing cabinet and removed the file drawer. There it was a small envelope taped to the back of the cabinet drawer with a key and six numbers on a slip of paper. I put the envelope and key in my pocket and started putting everything back. I didn't want anyone after me to know I had searched the place. Just as I was finishing, I heard someone coming down the hall. I walked over and turned off the light and stood near the hinged side of the door with my back against the wall. I heard a key go into the lock and unlock the door; it started to open. They turned on the light. Standing behind the door, I could see through the space between the door and doorframe; a woman was entering the room. She was short, maybe 5'2" slim and blond. From the back, all I could see she was wearing was a black skirt and black jacket.

She entered and closed the door. With her back to me, I said, "Hello, are you looking for me?"

She turned with a startled look.

"Who are you?"

"I am Warren Steelgrave, but I think you know that. It's your turn, lady. Who are you, and what are you doing here?"

With an attitude, she said, "I don't know who you are. I'm Sandra Moretti. I'm here because I was asked by the family to come by and get Mauro's personal things."

I took out my phone and snapped a quick photo of her.

"Let me send this to Signor Moretti and see what he thinks."

In a panic, she responded, "Please don't. I am Sandra Rovetto. I was very close to Mauro; our relationship was very private. I knew he had this secret office. Some men have my mother and made me tell them of this place. I came to make sure there was nothing of mine left here."

"When did you tell them of this office?"

"Maybe half an hour ago."

"I suggest you get out of here as fast as you can."

With that said, I left. As I started down the hall, I heard the elevator start. I went past the elevator to the stairs and started down. Then, I stopped on the third step and waited. I heard the elevator doors open; someone got out and started down the hall, away from the stairs. I stepped up two steps and looked around the corner down the hall. Two men stopped at room 225, and they tried the door. It was still unlocked: they went in. I thought for a moment what to do. Were they Moretti's men or Aashiq's men? I decided to wait. After about fifteen minutes, all three came out of the room and left. As they waited for the elevator, I made my way down the stairs and out of the building. I was going to follow them, then thought, why? I have the key.

I had passed a restaurant coming from the station, *La Pasta*. I decided to head back there to think about what to do next. I entered the restaurant. It was a typical layout, a small counter and cash register near the door on the left as you entered. A counter with seating for eight on the right and tables for four throughout the rest of the restaurant. I was seated near a front window. It was not very large, but it was very clean, and the aromas were wonderful.

While I was waiting for my food, I decided to find out who the owner of the building was; maybe he had some answers on the key. I took out my phone and started searching for a real estate agent in Lucca. I called the first one on the list.

"Pronto"

"*Ciao. Mi scusi, parla inglese?*"

"Yes. How can I help you?"

"My name is Warren Steelgrave, and I want to rent some office space. I passed by a building at 255 Via del Peso and was wondering if there was any space there for rent."

"I can contact the owner. My name is Carlo Ponte, Mr. Steelgrave; how can I reach you?"

I gave him my phone number and explained I was on my way back to Florence and would be in town for only a couple of more hours. Just then, my lunch arrived.

I had finished my lunch, and as the waitress set down a cup of coffee, my phone began to vibrate. It was Carlo.

"The owner has a space that is coming up for rent. He can meet us at the building in fifteen minutes."

"I will be there, Carlo. A presto."

Chapter 16

I FINISHED MY COFFEE, paid my check, and headed back to the office building. When I arrived at the building, two men were standing out front. Both were middle age. One had a very loud sports coat over a white shirt and was wearing jeans with running shoes. Must be the real estate agent. The other was wearing jeans and a collared pink pullover shirt. As I approached, the one in the loud jacket stepped forward with an outstretched hand and a smile. "Mr. Steelgrave?"

I nodded and shook his hand.

"I'm, Carlo Ponte. And this is, Signor Martini. He has a small office on the second floor that will be available at the end of the month. The tenant has not moved out yet, but he would like to show it to you. He says it fits the description of what you said your needs were."

I shook Signor Martini's hand, He unlocked the front door of the building, and we all went in. We got into the elevator and got out on the second floor. I followed behind as we went down the hall. He stopped at 225 and inserted a key to unlock the door. We all went in, and to Signor Martini's surprise, the room was in shambles. All the drawers in the desk were pulled out, and the files were stacked on the floor next to a wall. The desk was taken apart, and I could see the tape that held the key still partially hanging on the back of one file drawer. Signor Martini, turned to me trying to recover from the surprise, and said, "I guess the tenant is already in the process of moving."

I just nodded and then looked over the room as if I was deciding to take it, then said, "Let me think about it. I will let you know by morning."

I collected a business card from each, and we left the building. We said our goodbyes in front of the building, and I walked away. I was walking back to *La Pasta* and thinking. Signor Martini was involved somehow; how else would he know the office would be vacant soon? He knew Mauro wasn't coming back. He was the only one that knew for sure. I arrived at *La Pasta* and went in. I stood just inside, waiting to be seated when the waitress noticed me and walked up with a seductive smile.

"You came back. I was hoping I would see you again."

She led me to a table in the back and asked if I needed another menu.

"No. Just a glass of wine, red, please."

She smiled and left to retrieve my wine. I started thinking through all the ways Signor Martini could be involved. I decided I would ask him. I took out my phone and called him.

"Pronto."

"Signor Martini, this is Warren Steelgrave is it possible I meet you at the office for one more look? My partner asked I take a picture with my phone and send it to him."

"Certainly, I can meet you there in about thirty minutes."

"Good. See you then."

I put my phone away just as the waitress returned with my wine. She sat it down with a folded piece of paper. Before she walked away, I said, "Is it possible for me to purchase a complete roll of two-euro coins?"

She looked puzzled, nodded, and said, "Certainly." Then left.

I opened the folded paper: Her name and phone number.

She returned with my coins, and I asked, "Catherina, what time do you get off work?"

"At 6:00."

"Dinner?"

"Your name," she asked with a tilt of the head and an inquisitive look?

"Warren Steelgrave," I said with a smile. "You decide where and time."

"OK. You call me."

I finished my wine, picked up the coins off the table, and put it in my pocket with a napkin. I paid my bill and left to meet Signor Martini. When I got there, it was starting to get dark and beginning to cool off. There was a slight breeze picking up, and it had a sharpness to it. I walked up to the glass door, and Signor Martini was waiting inside. He stepped forward and opened the door for me, and we headed for the elevator. When we reached the office, he unlocked it, and I followed him into the office. I closed the door behind me and stood there waiting for him to turn.

My hand was in my pocket wrapped with the napkin and clutching the roll of coins. When Signor Martini turned to face me, he was pulling a gun out of his pocket. Just as the gun was about to get clear of the pocket, I stepped forward and hit him in the face as hard as I could with my fist clutching the coins. He dropped like a ton of bricks.

When he came to, I had his gun and was going through his pockets. He got to one knee and, after a few moments, managed to get to his feet, holding a very swollen right jaw: it was broken.

He stood there looking rather pitiful. I could almost feel sorry for him if it wasn't for the fact, he tried to pull a gun on me. "OK, Signor Martini, why the gun?"

He just stood there and shrugged his shoulders. I was impatient and started toward him to balance the swelling on the other side of his face. He held up a hand, signaling for me to give him a second. Then he started speaking.

"I got a call just after you left telling me to keep an eye on the place. They said they would make it worth my while if I called them and kept the person here until they came for him or her. I had just ended the call when you called. I thought I would meet with you and use the gun to keep you here until they arrived."

"Have you called them?"

"No. I wanted to make sure you got here and didn't change your mind."

"Who were they, Martini?"

"I don't know. After seeing the room that had been ransacked, I assumed they didn't find what they were looking for and wanted information from anyone that came looking for the same thing."

I thought for a moment and decided that his story hung together enough to trust that it was mostly true, then I continued with what I had come back for. I started by asking how long Mauro Moretti had rented the space, and on and on. I questioned him for about a half-hour. I was convinced of two things. First, his only involvement was renting the office to Mauro, and second, he hadn't talked with Mauro about a second office that the key in my pocket was for. Then just as he thought we were through and he was starting to leave, I surprised him by saying, "How did you know Mauro was dead, and the office was available?"

I watched closely for his tell as he answered, "Dead? I did not know he was dead. He was late on the rent, and he was never late. I called the number on the rental agreement, and a woman answered. I asked for him and was told he left town and wasn't coming back."

I was convinced that was the truth. I told Martini to keep quiet about me being there and left.

I stood in the lobby, looking through the glass door up and down the street. When I was convinced no one was watching the building, I stepped out onto the street and started walking towards *La Pasta*. I looked at my watch; it was almost 6:00. I dialed Catherina's number, wondering if it was a real number. She answered.

"Pronto."

"Catherina? It's Warren. Dinner?"

"I am just leaving to go home; pick me up in twenty minutes. I just want to change clothes. I will text you the address."

Chapter 17

I CHECKED THE ADDRESS I received on Google maps; It was about a twenty-minute walk. I decided to not take a taxi. I would walk using the time to think. Who did Martini call that told him Mauro was not coming back? It had to be someone who knew about the office. Someone who knew Mauro wasn't coming back to the office. They must have already searched it. Someone in the Moretti family. How else would I have been sent the key? Had they missed the key behind the drawer, or was it planted there on purpose?

I got to the apartment address and walked up to the large front door. I pushed the button next to her name, and out of the speaker, a voice said, "I will be right down."

After a few moments, the door opened, and she stepped out. She had changed clothes and was wearing black leggings with a black mini skirt, white blouse, red flats, and a gray jacket with a multicolored scarf. She was wearing her hair down and not up as she did in the restaurant. It cascaded from under a gray knitted woolen cap to beyond her shoulders framing her face. It was like looking at a

painting in a museum the way it drew you into her eyes.
Large hazel eyes: she was stunning. She smiled, breaking
my trance. She was pleased with my reaction, then said,
"We will need a taxi. There is a taxi stand this way just
around the corner."

I smiled and nodded in that direction, and we were off.
We arrived at La Tana del Bola near the Piazza San Michele
and got out. As we entered the restaurant, I reached in my
pocket for the security of my coins. The restaurant was
small and rustic with a warm feeling. We were seated in
the back at a small table out of the way and intimate. It was
more a sandwich shop and not a restaurant. In the States,
we would call it a wine bar.

"Hope you don't mind. I hardly ever eat a full meal in
the evening."

"Not at all, Catherina." This was my kind of girl.

We ordered a bottle of wine and a platter of different
cheeses and meats to share. The perfect meal to induce
conversation and a kind of intimacy. We ate, talked,
and laughed for hours. Catherina was thirty-two and
a graduate from the University of Florence. Then she
let me in on something she was holding back. She had
recognized me when I walked into the restaurant. She
had been a guest at the party I attended with Maria.
She had arrived late. She was friends of the writer, Jack,
the fellow who introduced me to Absinthe and got there
just as I was leaving.

"So, you have had me at a disadvantage all evening. You
have seen me at my worst," I said.

"If that was your worst, it was not so bad," she said with
a slight smile and mischievous look.

She was an art major, working in her dad's restaurant with hopes of opening an art gallery someday.

I looked at my watch; it was getting late. I said we better go, I didn't know when the last train to Florence was. Then I got an idea. I took a picture out of my wallet of Mauro and showed it to her.

"Have you seen this man before?" I asked

"Yes. That is Mauro Moretti. I have seen him twice in the restaurant. Once with a man, he was arguing with. Why?"

"I have something of his I want to return to him. I went to his office today and was told he had moved and wasn't coming back and left no forwarding address. How do you know him?"

"I have never met him. Everyone knows who the members of the Moretti family are. You don't want to do or say something they might think is disrespectful." She was looking very curiously at me, and I felt I needed to explain, to ease any concerns.

"Catherina, I am trying to find Mauro Moretti for his uncle, who has concerns over his safety. Do you think he might have another place no one knows about where I might find him?"

"No."

"Be careful, Warren, I have read your books. I went to the party in hopes of meeting you. You tend to get in over your head."

I smiled and said, "Let's go. It's getting late, and I don't want to miss the train."

We left the restaurant and took a taxi back to her apartment.

"Would you like to come up?"

"No, Catherina, I really have to go."

"Warren, will I see you again?"

"Yes, I will call, and we can spend a day in the city. I have always wanted to tour Lucca with a local."

With that, she headed into her apartment. The taxi driver was waiting for further instructions.

"Is it possible for you to drive me to Florence?"

"Yes."

"Take me to the Santa Maria Novella train station."

He looked into the rear-view mirror, and our eyes met. He nodded, and we were off. By now, Sandra Rovetto would have told the men that took her that I had left the office just before they arrived. They would be watching the train station and bus station and my apartment. I would stay the night in a hotel near the station and rent a car in the morning. I needed to talk with the woman who told Signor Martini that Mauro wasn't coming back. It had to be someone in the Moretti family, the person who knew of the office and had the key that was given to me. In the morning, I would get a message to Signor Moretti, telling him I was on my way and needed to talk with the person who knew about the office.

We drove for about one hour and thirty minutes, and he let me out at the station. I walked to the *Le Stanza Del Medici* hotel and got a room for the night. I laid in bed, thinking through the events of the day. Aashiq, having taken the girl, now knows I might have information. I would be abducted the first chance Aashiq's men had. I should have brought my backpack."

Chapter 18

I GOT UP AND showered, put on yesterday's clothes, and checked out. I headed over to the Café Duomo for a Cappuccino and a brioche. I walked in and sat near a window in front where I could watch the street. Mauro came over.

"Buongiorno, Warren."

"Buongiorno, Mauro. A Cappuccino and a brioche, please."

He nodded and left to get my coffee.

I sat thinking. They won't be following me any longer: They are going to abduct me. The girl must have told them I was in the office, and they figured out I left with something. I must get into my rented apartment and retrieve my backpack. It had my passport satellite phone and a change of clothes. I had packed it as a go-bag just in case, I had to make a quick exit. Aashiq's men would be watching the building; I was sure I would get in, but getting out would be the problem.

Mauro returned with my order.

"Mauro, can you get a message to Signor Moretti?"

"Yes."

"Tell him I'm coming to see him. I need to talk to him about the key."

Mauro nodded and left.

I finished my coffee; on my way out, Mauro came up to me and said, "He will be waiting for you at his home."

"Thanks, Mauro."

I got to within three blocks of the apartment and started looking for suspicious activity and people. I didn't see any but knew they were there. Just as I got to the corner of my block, a bus turned the corner and stopped between the corner and my front door. I stepped up my pace and blended in with the crowd getting off the bus. I got to the front door of the building and unlocked it and went in. I wasn't fooling myself; they would be right behind me as soon as the small crowd dispersed some.

I unlocked the door to my apartment and leaving the door open. I went in and grabbed my backpack. I went back out through the door, closing and locking it. I started for the stairs and heard someone ringing all the tenant's doorbells. Just as I got to the second landing, I heard the door unlatch and people coming in. I headed as fast as I could for the roof.

At the top of the stairs, I went through a door and onto the roof. I surveyed the roof. There was a make-shift ladder going over the edge at one end. For sure, someone was at the bottom guarding for the escape. On the opposite side of the roof was a building separated from this building by a small alley. It had a flat roof ringed with a two-foot parapet. I ran over to the edge; the distance was about eight feet. I heaved my backpack with all the strength I had: it cleared the parapet and landed on the roof. Now it was my turn. Ten years ago, this would not be a problem, but today it would be iffy. I stepped back and jumped for it. I slammed into the wall hard and grabbed onto the parapet. I threw my right leg over the parapet, and pulling myself over fell onto the roof. Lying flat on the roof behind the parapet, I heard the door open, and men step out onto the other roof. My plan was; that if they decided to make the same jump, I would stand and knock them down the six floors into the alley.

After they surveyed the roof, I heard one say

"He must of went into an apartment on the way up. Let's go, we can search each one on the way down."

When I heard the door shut, I quickly found the roof access to this building. I got lucky it wasn't completely closed. I made my way down to the street and disappeared around the corner.

I walked for maybe five blocks before I found a taxi. I had him take me to Avis car rental near the airport, where I rented a Fiat 500. As I left the city on my way to Cremona, it occurred to me how little time I had before these guys caught up to me.

Just then, that satellite phone rang. It was Jim: I answered.
"Hello"

"Warren, I have some information I needed to talk to you about. A body of a young woman turned up today 5'2" blonde, slim and at onetime attractive. She must be involved somehow. She was tortured in the same way as Mauro. They used a hot clothes iron on the souls of her feet and beat her to a pulp. We are trying to identify her, but it will take some time. I wanted to get this to you to add to anything you have gathered."

"Sandra Rovetto"

"What?" responded Jim

"I think she is, Sandra Rovetto, Mauro's mistress. I came across her searching a hidden office Mauro had."

"You are supposed to give me such information, Warren!"

"I just did, Jim. I have been a little busy. I will call you later."

I hung up. Jim saved my life, and it wasn't I didn't trust him; it was I didn't trust the FBI. Then I called Signor Moretti on the satellite phone. I told him to expect me around noon.

I arrived at Signor Moretti's house. I drove down the long private drive and into the circular driveway, parking in front of the front door. I got out and walked to the door and rang the bell. The door opened, and I was greeted by Gino. I thought to myself, "Who dresses this guy" He always looks as if he just stepped off the cover of GQ magazine. "Good afternoon, Mr. Steelgrave, Signor Moretti is waiting for you in the library."

I followed Gino to the library and walked in. Moretti was standing at the small table in the middle of the room, pouring himself a drink. Setting in one of two wingback chairs to the right of the table and near a wall was a woman I did not recognize. "Would you like a drink, Mr. Steelgrave?"

"Thank you. I would: Bourbon neat."

"Let me introduce my daughter-in-law, Sabrina."

Sabrina rose as I walked over and extended a hand to shake. Signor Moretti motioned with his hand that I take a seat in the matching wingback chair, and I sat down. Then he began.

"Sabrina was the person who had the key."

I turned my attention to her. She was very nervous and a little embarrassed as she began her story.

"Mr. Steelgrave, please forgive my English." I nodded, and she continued. "I had suspicions for a while that Mauro had a lover. I hired a man to follow him: Signor Larice. He followed him to that office to meet with a woman. Several days later, Mauro came home and was nervous. He said he had to go out, which made me mad. He was getting ready, and I searched his coat and found the key and took it. I thought it would serve him good to meet her and not be able to get into the office. He never returned. That was the last I ever saw or heard from him. Then I received a call about the rent. I told the caller Mauro was gone."

"May I have the information on the man you hired to follow Mauro?"

She had anticipated the question and handed me the information. I sat there without anything else to ask her. Signor Moretti gave her a nod, and she left the room. Then he turned to me and said, "Mr. Steelgrave, if you haven't yet, soon you will realize you and your family will never be safe until Aashiq is dead. Finding the protocol will not end it. He will torture you to death to find out what you had found out. He will torture those around you to get you. I have had my men looking for him. He is very allusive and smart; we cannot find a clue. You are the one who will have to get it done. He is, after all, after you; you don't have to look for him. I know you like to keep information to yourself, but if I were you, I would let me help you."

I sat finishing my drink then stood; shaking his hand, I said, "I do understand, and you will be the first I will let know when I get a lead on him."

I turned and left.

Chapter 19

I GOT IN MY car and drove to an Osteria I had passed on my way through town. I was getting a little hungry and needed time to plan what to do next. I went in and was seated at a small table near a back wall. I got there just before they closed at 3:00 p.m. It had a red brick arched ceiling that was very beautiful. After I gave my order to the waitress, I started thinking of what to do next.

I took out of my pocket the information Sabrina had given me: Signor Larice. His address was in Lucca. I guess I will be headed back to Lucca. I was thinking, "How do I approach this guy? Had Mauro mentioned him to Sandra Rovetto, and she gave it up to her torturers? Had they gotten to him and are waiting for me. That is what I would do." Just then, my meal came. Something will come to me: I think better on a full stomach.

I took out my phone and made a reservation at a hotel in Lucca. Next, I called Catherina.

"Hello?"

"Catherina, it's Warren. I have to come to Lucca tonight on some business. You free for dinner again?" There was

a long pause then she answered,

"What time, Warren?"

"You tell me, I have a car, and I can pick you up where and when you want."

"I have a meeting with a man about a gallery space after closing. You can come by the restaurant say 9:00 this evening,"

"OK."

I checked my watch for the time. I had time to get to the hotel in Lucca and freshen up a little before going over to the restaurant to pick up Catherina.

I arrived at the restaurant just before 9:00 p.m. As I walked up to the door, I could see through the main window that Catherina was having an intense discussion with a gentleman about forty-five years old. I paused outside, not wanting to interrupt. In just a moment or two, I could tell from Catherina's facile expressions and body language she felt threatened. Having had a business for thirty years, this was all too familiar. I had fired some very talented men for this type of behavior. They would use their position of power or advantage to intimidate women into performing sexual favors. It was never a problem in the field with the construction workers. They had as much disrespect for this type of weak men as I did.

We had many women in our crews, and if someone tried this, they would have the shit beat out of them.

I knocked on the locked door. Catherina looked over and, with a relieved look on her face, started for the door. She unlocked the door, and I walked in. The gentleman turned and looking perturbed, said goodnight and left.

"What was that all about?"

"Nothing, Warren, just men being men."

Two things upset me about this kind of situation. First, women do not want to talk about it, and if you pursue the subject, you look like a jealous jerk. Second, the word men. I hate being lumped in with guys like that.

"Come on, Warren, let's go. Where do you want to have dinner?"

"I would like to go to the same place as last night."

She smiled and nodded, and we were off to dinner. At dinner, I steered the conversation to the guy giving her a bad time.

"Catherina, have you found a place for your gallery?"

"I thought so, but maybe it isn't right."

"Rent too high?"

"Yes."

"Where is it located?"

Her eyes lit up with excitement as she started talking about it.

"It's just across the piazza from here. It's the perfect location and size." Then she paused, and her demeanor dampened as she went on. "But it might be a bigger problem than I thought with the landlord. He has a ceramic shop next door. I don't think I can trust he won't keep demanding higher and higher rents."

"I understand, Catherina." Changing the subject, I went on. "I have a favor to ask."

"Sure, Warren."

I handed her the small paper with the name and address of the private eye I had received from Sabrina.

"I would like for you to arrange a meeting for me with this man. Tell him Sabrina Moretti needs to meet with him. Give him this restaurant as the meeting place. I will call you after you have met with him, I will let the phone ring twice and hang up. I will call right back. You will not see a phone number. The phone is encrypted."

She raised an eyebrow, and with a suspicious look, said, "Warren, why all the intrigue?"

"I wish I could tell you that you weren't putting yourself in danger, but I can't lie to you. It's dangerous. If you do this, you and I can't see or talk to each other until this business is finished. I'm searching for Mauro Moretti and think others are searching for him also. This gentleman, I believe, has a lead that I need. Don't tell him anything about yourself: Nothing. Give him the note and leave. I will make sure you are not followed."

She agreed to hunt him down in the morning then asked, "How will I get ahold of you to let you know I have met with him?"

"I will know. I will be watching to make sure you're safe."

After dinner, we walked across the piazza and looked into the windows of the space she had hoped would be her new gallery.

"Catherina, this is a great space. It will have a lot of foot traffic."

Staring into the gallery space through the window, and in a low defeated sounding voice, she said, "I am not sure I can work out my differences with the owner."

She turned to Warren, and he was smiling.

"Catherina, keep a good thought. I am sure you will come to an agreement with the owner on terms that you will like. It's late, let me get you home."

Chapter 20

I AWOKE THE NEXT morning and went straight over to Catherina's apartment after stopping for a large coffee, croissant, and a bottle of water. I parked my car on a side street where I could watch for her to leave. I sat sipping my water, and after about an hour, I watched as she stepped out of the apartment and onto the street. She turned left and started walking towards the taxi stand. There was no one on the street; she wasn't being followed.

I trailed her across Lucca. The taxi stopped in front of a small ancient building on a crowded street. I could not tell what kind of business occupied it. The private investigator must share an office. She got out of the taxi and had it wait while she went in. In less than five minutes, she came out and left. I waited and could tell no one was following her. I took out the encrypted phone and called her. Two rings and I hung up. Then I called back.

"Hello"

"Did it go, OK?"

"Yes. Signor Larice will meet you at 8:00 p.m."

"Thanks, Catherina. I will see you in a few weeks."

"Warren, what if I need to see you before then?"

"Leave word with Signor Moretti. He will contact me."

I ended the call and looked at my watch; it was 9:00. The ceramic shop would be opening soon. I started the car and drove to the piazza. I parked the car on a side street a block away. I walked to a small coffee bar on the piazza and ordered a cappuccino. I took my coffee and sat at a table that gave me a view of the front of the ceramic shop.

I was just finishing my coffee when the owner appeared, unlocked the front door, and went in. Perfect timing. I got up, walked over, and entered the shop. It was a small shop with ceramic platters on the walls with umbrella stands, large vases, and such on the floor. The owner was standing behind a small counter and looked up from what he was doing as I entered.

I could tell he recognized me from last night. He was concerned as well as he should be. I walked straight to the counter with a purpose in my stride. The closer I got, the wider his eyes became. When I stopped at the counter, his eyes were the size of silver dollars. Looking straight into them, I began, "*Parli Inglese?*" He nodded, yes. "Good, I don't want to be misunderstood. Signor Moretti would be every upset if I told him what happened last night." His eyes filled with fear. "You will call Catherina and tell her you thought it over, and a gallery would be perfect for next door. It would bring in a lot of foot traffic for your shop. Understand?" He nodded again. "What was the rent payment you discussed with her?"

"Eight hundred euros a month."

"The rent will be six hundred euros a month and free the first three months; understood?" Slowly he nodded yes. "Are you questioning this arrangement?" I took out my phone and said. "If you like, I can call Signor Moretti, and you can negotiate better terms with him." He held out both hands, palms out, shaking his head no. A man of little words I like that.

"One last thing. If it gets back to me that any part of this agreement is broken or Catherina feels threatened in any way by anybody, I assure you, someone will pay you a visit, and you won't want that. Are we clear?" He nodded, yes. "Are we clear!!"

"Yes."

"Thank you." I smiled and left. I went back to my room to wait out the day until my meeting with Signore Larice. I wanted to stay off the streets. I know I am being hunted.

I sat at the small table in front of the window, looking out, watching for any suspicious activity on the street. I took out the envelope with the key and slip of paper with the six numbers. I started with the key first. Studying the key, it was obvious it was not to any door lock, but maybe a padlock. Turning my attention to the numbers, they could not be a phone number, not enough numbers. It had to be a password code to something. I got to the restaurant just before 8:00 that evening and walked in.

"*Buonasera signore, uno per cena?*"

"No. I will be meeting someone, a Signor Larice. May we have a table in the back?" She smiled and directed me to follow her; I followed her to a small table in the back corner of the restaurant. I ordered antipasti and a bottle of Barbara.

Just after the food arrived, the hostess was headed to my table with a man in tow. He didn't fit the image of a private detective I had. If I had an image of an Italian private detective. He was, I would guess, in his late forties, well dressed in a gray suit, white shirt, and an expensive red tie. A great cover for someone lurking around following a person. As he arrived at the table, I stood to shake his hand.

"Buonasera, Signor Larice."

"Good evening Mr. . . . ?"

"Steelgrave, thank you for coming. Your English is very good."

"I was told I would be meeting Sabrina Moretti?"

"Sorry, she won't be coming."

Mr. Larice pulled out his chair, and while he was sitting down, he responded, "I was born and raised in the States. Tell me, Mr. Steelgrave, why all the cloak and dagger?"

I offered a glass of wine, and he nodded yes. As I poured the wine, I answered, "I was asked by the Moretti family to locate Mauro Moretti, who has gone missing. I think he has information a terrorist group wants; he was abducted on his way to an office he kept secret from his wife. In this office, he kept a key and a numeric code, which is where the information is kept. He never got to the office to retrieve it.

Sabrina Moretti told me she hired you to follow him. She told me in your report to her; you told her about the office. Where else might he had gone that would need a key and a code?"

Signor Larice reached for a breadstick and his wine to give himself a chance to think. He was not sure how he found himself in such a mess. He only agreed to meet because he thought he was being interviewed by a new client. He concluded Sabrina had given Steelgrave his name, and he had no choice but to give him what he wants.

"Mr. Steelgrave, there was one place. It was a small storage facility where you could rent small closet type spaces by the month. It has a front entry door that required you to use a passcode to enter the facility. It was located near the other office on the same side of the street, half a block south. I followed him one night. He went in but didn't stay very long, left, and went home. I did not think much about it, many businesses store old records in such a place."

Chapter 21

W E FINISHED OUR wine and stood to leave. I reached over and shook his hand and said, "Thanks for the information. I need to leave, have a pleasant rest of the evening Signor Larice."

He smiled and said, "Also you, Mr. Steelgrave; I will just use *le toilette* before I go."

I smiled, nodded, and left. I stood outside the restaurant buttoning my coat, deciding to go by the storage facility tonight or tomorrow when it's light. I decided the sooner, the better. It's only a matter of time before the terrorists turn up here in Lucca looking for me. I drove over to within a block of Mauro's secret office and parked on a side street. I got out of the car and found a doorway to stand in. The night was getting cold and damp. I stood observing the area looking for anybody suspicious watching the office building. I checked every doorway and small alley: No one.

I stepped out of the doorway and started up the street, staying in the shadows as much as possible. This part of the town was deserted. Soon I came across a small two-story building between two larger buildings. It looked as if it was a small store of some kind with a residence above. Its front door had a keypad entry.

I walked to the door and punched in the code. The door unlocked. I opened the door, walked in, and quickly closed it behind me. There was a small night light that gave a slight lumination to the area I was standing in. I stood there, allowing my eyes to adjust to the dim light. Looking around, I saw a light switch near the door to my right. I reached over and turned on the lights.

The whole area was divided up into cubicles of different sizes with cyclone fencing from floor to ceiling, with a locked gate as an entrance to each cubicle. They were filled with a variety of things, from bikes to bed headboards. Most had banker file boxes storing files. "Which one was his?" I thought. I walked up to the first one and found a tag in front, identifying it with four numbers. I started walking down isles, looking at the tags until I came to one that matched the last four numbers of the password. Putting the key in the lock, it unlocked.

It was a small cubicle only four feet wide by eight feet deep: it had only one four-drawer file cabinet. I opened the bottom drawer; it was empty. Same with the next drawer up. The third drawer up from the bottom was half full. Looking quickly at the files, they all seemed to be old business records. The top file was more interesting; aside from old business files, there were files with copies of emails and memos. What would a file of protocols look like, I had no idea, but it had to be in this small cubicle.

Then I got an idea. I took out a batch of files and file hangers and set them on top of the cabinet. Lying flat at the bottom of the drawer was a file folder. I picked it up and thumbed through it. This had to be it. I looked at each sheet of paper, and although it was written describing stuff, I had no idea of. I could tell it was a detailed step by step directions.

I replaced the files I had taken out, relocked the cubicle, and made my way to the front door. Standing at the door, I reached over and turned off the lights. Next, I prepared mentally for opening the door and finding a couple of terrorists waiting for me to leave. I opened the door and stepped onto the street: No one. The street was deserted. I walked back to my car and drove back to my hotel. I parked, got out of the car, and started walking the two blocks to the hotel. Two men stepped out of a darkened doorway. I immediately placed the file folder in my waistband at the small of my back, turned, and started running. I was running for my life, and they were younger and gaining on me. I turned down an alley, hoping to find an unlocked door to a building that I could duck into; I found nothing. Worse, as I approached the far end of the alley, it was closed off.

I turned just as they entered the alley. When the two men could see I had no way out, they slowed to a walk to catch their breath. I frantically looked around for something I could use as a weapon. I found a piece of wood about two feet long and two by two inches square.

The two men spread apart by three feet. One pulled a knife and began to smile. He appeared to be about five foot eight inches with dark hair. It was hard to tell his age because of a face only a mother could love. It was scarred from many fights. The second man was about the same height not as ugly but a meaner sadistic look. He would enjoy brutalizing me. He pulled out a small pistol.

Just as they got close, I heard a muffled sound, and the one with the gun fell to the ground. At the same time, the one with the knife glanced over to his friend as he was falling. I didn't hesitate; I stepped forward and swung my piece of wood as hard as I could. I hit him alongside his head. That didn't drop him, but it had enough force to cause him to drop the knife and stagger. I wasted no time pushing him against the wall of the alley, pummeling his face. With his head tight against the wall, each strike caused the maximum amount of damage. When I finished, he slid down the wall and lay on the ground.

I turned and saw Piero going through the pockets of the other man. I walked over and asked, "How is he?"

"Dead," was his answer.

"Thanks, Piero. I was having visions of being strapped down and a hot iron being put to the bottom of my feet. Do you have a plan for the body?"

"Yes. That will be no problem. What about the other one? I bet he knows the location of Aashiq."

"Piero, I want to take him somewhere and question him. I need to cut the head off the snake."

Piero nodded; he knew what I was referring to; as long as Aashiq was alive, I would be in danger.

Chapter 22

PIERO LEFT TO go get his car leaving me there to keep an eye on the one that was alive. After what seemed like an eternity, he backed down the alley in his car. Leaving the car running, he got out, and I helped him put the body in the trunk. He kept looking over at the other man that was just lying there on his side. After we got the body into the trunk of the car, Piero took out a roll of duct tape and started over to the man lying on the ground. When he got there, his head twitched a little with surprise. He turned to me and said, "I was wondering why he didn't get up and run away or yell. Who taught you to use his shoelaces to bind his hands and feet and to stuff his sock in his mouth?"

"Just seemed logical he wouldn't stay semiconscious for long, and I was not going to fight him again."

Piero replaced the sock and shoelaces with duct tape. After stuffing him into the trunk of Piero's car, he turned to me and said, "Go get your car and follow me. I have a place we can take him. He will tell us what we want to know."

I nodded OK and left to go get my car. I got to my car and unlocked it and got in. The first thing I did was to remove the file from my waistband and slid it under the seat.

When I drove back, Piero was parked on the street waiting for me. I pulled alongside his car, and when he saw it was me, he nodded and pulled away from the curb.

I followed him through the city, and soon we were headed through the walls of the city and out to the countryside. After about twenty minutes, we arrived at an old, abandoned industrial building. As we started down the long driveway, Piero flashed his lights. A large roll-up door on the side of the building began to open. We drove down alongside the building and through the opened door and into the building. The door began to close as soon as we both were inside.

Several men were waiting, and as soon as we stopped the car, without saying a word, they walked over. Piero popped the trunk, and two men dragged the man out of the trunk and over to an inverted wood table at the other end of the building. "They are going to waterboard him," I thought.

I walked over to Piero and said, "Waterboarding?"

"It's not as sadistic as what he would have done to you, but more effective; after we will shoot him. Anything you need to know?"

"Just the location of Aashiq, and how many bodyguards." Then I walked over to a man-door that was next to the rollup door and went outside.

The night air was cold, and there was no moon making it very dark. As I leaned up against the wall of the building, I felt my cigar case in my pocket and remembered I had one cigar left. I took it out and lit it. I could hear muffled screams from inside the building, and it was making me uncomfortable. After about forty-five minutes, the sounds stopped. Piero came out; he shrugged his shoulders and said, "He has passed out. We will give him a few minutes and start again. He is a tough one; this could take hours."

I looked at my cigar then replied, "I will wait and finish my cigar; about twenty more minutes. If you haven't finished by then, I will leave and wait for your call. Signor Moretti has the number."

He nodded; he understood and went back in. I leaned back against the wall finishing my cigar and thinking what to do next. Just as I finished my cigar and the muffled screams began again. I went back into the building and walked to my car. Inside the car, I took out the ID, I had taken off the terrorist after I tied him up with the shoelaces. I took out my iPhone, took a picture of it and texted it and my satellite phone number and the phone number I wrote down from the terrorist's phone to my friend Jim Marino with a note to call me. I started the car; Piero raised the door, and I headed back to my room. Once there, I put the file in my backpack for safekeeping.

Jim and I have been friends for over thirty years. We met when I was still in business and he was a police chief. He was just under six feet tall; he was trim and fit with chiseled features and deep blue eyes at sixty-seven; he was still very good-looking. As police chief, he had made many contacts in high places and at homeland security. Ten years back, he started a security agency. His company would give security protection for diplomats and high-level executives of multinational companies.

My Satellite phone began to buzz. I looked at my watch; it was almost 2:00 a.m. 7:00 p.m. on the west coast of America. I answered, "Hello."

"Warren? It's Jim. What the hell is going on? I hate getting clandestine messages at 2:00 a.m. your time. What's up?"

I started at the beginning and explained the whole situation I was in. I asked Jim to get me all the information he could on the ID I sent him and all recent phone calls from the cell number I had sent.

"Warren, wouldn't it be quicker to have the FBI do it?"

"It would, Jim, if I could trust them. If I give them the file, I'm not sure it wouldn't be leaked that they have it. I might lose the protection of Signor Moretti. As it is right now, both the FBI and Signor Moretti have a vested interest in me staying alive and not captured until I find it. It was Signor Moretti's men that saved me tonight. I am sure the FBI was close as well. My only use to the FBI after they have the file is to use me as bait to catch Aashiq, the leader of *Allah's Army*. That could involve me being picked up and tortured for a while."

There was silence for a time. Then Jim replied, "Give me a day, and I will get back to you."

"Thanks, Jim."

***

Aashiq turned to Dabir, "Why don't Erol or Mohamed answer their phone?'

Dabir was on the computer and said.

"I just checked Steelgrave's phone. He has turned it on briefly from twenty kilometers outside the city."

"Outside the city? He must have given them the slip and is headed back to Florence."

"Dabir, we need to find Erol and Mohamed."

"I have already sent two men to their last location, a hotel in Lucca, and should hear from them shortly."

Just then, Dabir's phone started to buzz. He picked it up and looking at the screen said, "It's them, Aashiq," and answered the phone.

Aashiq could only listen to one side of the call, but it was clear Erol and Mohamed weren't there. Then Dabir said, "I am going to send you the coordinates for Warren Steelgrave's last phone location. They must have followed him. Go to the location and report back." He hung up the phone and looked over to Aashiq with a concerned face. Aashiq responded,

"This is not good."

Chapter 23

DABIR AND AASHIQ waited nervously for two of their men to get to the last known location of Steelgrave's phone. When they got there, they called Dabir.

"Hello."

"Dabir, we have arrived and parked on the side of the road. The coordinates you gave us are down a long driveway. The only thing there is a large industrial building. I see no cars, but maybe they are inside?"

"This could be a trap. Better you stay out of sight somewhere. You can watch the building."

The two men drove down the street and turned the car around. From this vantage point, they could watch the side of the building with the rollup door and yet were far enough down the street that their dark car blended into the darkness. They got comfortable and settled in for what might be a long time.

Dabir looked over to Aashiq for his opinion as to what to do. Aashiq was sitting at a small table next to a window that looked out on the street. He took out his gold cigarette case and removed a Turkish cigarette. Lighting it and looking across the small dimly lit room to Dabir, he said, "I think, Steelgrave, led Erol and Mohamed into a trap. If not, where is their car? Steelgrave must have called someone to tell them the deed was done. That explains it."

"What do we do now, Aashiq?"

Aashiq taking a long drag on the cigarette and semi in thought, answered, "We will set our own trap and wait. They will get all the information out of Erol and Mohamed. The information they want most is my location, and they will get it. But we will be prepared for them."

Dabir, in deep thought, nodded slowly in agreement. "Let us first go to the country house and prepare it as if we are there inside, waiting for Mohamed and Erol. We will post only one guard. You and I, with some of the men, will wait in the small grove of trees across the small field at the back of the house."

The phone rang. It was Adeel.

"Aashiq, it's Adeel. We waited and saw no movement, so we cautiously approached the building. There were no sounds, so we went inside, it was empty with a chair at one end of the warehouse. There was a lot of fresh blood. I don't think we will ever see Mohamed or Erol again. What do you want us to do?"

"We will meet you at the country house."

***

I was lying on the bed in meditation when the satellite phone began to vibrate. I answered, "Hello."

"Mr. Steelgrave, it's Piero. Signor Moretti asked that I call you and give you the information we got from the captive.

He had given us a location of Aashiq. It is a farmhouse in the country, about two hours' drive from here." Piero paused to wait for a response.

"What's the plan, Piero?"

"We are going to go and avenge Mauro's death."

"When?"

"Now, of course."

"Wait for me. Don't do anything until I have had a chance to talk with Signor Moretti."

Piero hesitated then answered, "I will wait."

I hung up the phone and called Signor Moretti.

"Hello."

"Signor, Moretti, it's Warren Steelgrave."

"Yes, Mr. Steelgrave."

"I have just talked with Piero. You need to tell them to wait. I want to be with them when they go to the farmhouse. I'm waiting for information that will make sure we get the right person and all responsible for, Mauro."

There was a long pause, then Signor Moretti responded, "How long."

"It will be light in just a few hours. I think once they realize their friends are not coming back, they will all gather at the farmhouse to decide what to do. We should use the time to survey the area around the house and come up with our own plan. I think sometime after dark tomorrow."

There was a long pause as Signor Moretti thought through what I had said. Then finally he said, "OK. I will call Piero. After we have a place close to the farmhouse to meet, he will call you with that location."

He hung up the phone. I laid back down on the bed to think. If this Aashiq is as cunning as Jim Dempsey says he is, surely, he has figured out his men are not coming back, and he has become the prey. I wondered just how accurate the information is Piero got after torturing Erol. He might not really know the location. If it was accurate, Aashiq knows we are coming and will be waiting. This just has a wrong feel to it.

I laid there, trying to slow down my thoughts. Finally, I was able to slip into a meditative state until morning. I got up and showered. As I was finishing dressing, the satellite phone began to vibrate. It was Piero with the address to a café in a small village, only about two miles from the farmhouse. I left my room and drove to the café.

When I entered the café, it was obvious I was expected. The waitress smiled and nodded for me to follow her. We walked through the café and down a hall past the restrooms to a back room. She knocked twice, then opened the door and closing it as I walked past her into the room.

The room was about twenty feet wide by thirty feet long with a large conference type table and chairs around it. Piero was sitting at the far end of the table with ten other armed men sitting and standing around. A small armed army was my thought.

I walked over to Piero and sat in the only empty seat and said, "Piero, what is the situation, anything new."

"We have one man keeping an eye on the place. He says there is one guard posted. The guard is pretending to be a kind of groundskeeper. There's some movement in the house, but he can't tell how many are in there."

"Piero, do you have a pair of binoculars?" Piero nodded, yes. "Good, grab them, and you and I go check it out."

Chapter 24

DABIR WAS SITTING on the ground, leaning against a tree watching daybreak when he said to Aashiq, "I don't think they are coming. Maybe Steelgrave didn't get the information on where the country house is."

Aashiq sat thinking for a moment, then replied, "This Steelgrave is smart. He has figured that we have set a trap. He won't come until tonight. You stay here and wait. If I am wrong, you spring the trap. Adeel and I will leave through the woods. I will contact you as soon as I get settled somewhere else."

***

Piero and I walked out to the car and headed to the country house. About a mile from the location, we parked the car on the shoulder of the road and got out. Piero's lookout was farther down the road and viewing the house from the other direction. I took the binoculars and started surveying the area around the house. Then I said, "Piero, call and have the men gather here. We will approach the house from here." I handed the binoculars to Piero and continued. "See that small grove of trees? From here, we can move to the trees, which will give us a cover and closer surveillance of the house. Having not heard from the other two men, they have had to assume we are coming. I bet Aashiq has set a trap and is not there."

Piero nodded and took out his phone. Before he could make the call, the Carabinieri showed up in force and started down the long dusty driveway towards the house. Piero put away his phone. I thought, "FBI, I knew they were watching last night." I tapped Piero on the shoulder and pointed towards the back of the grove of trees. Four men were leaving across the field. I raised the binoculars and looked. One was lagging behind the others; he was wearing a red cap and was making a call. Excited, I said, "Piero lets go; the one in the red hat is in charge. If we hurry, we can catch him before he catches up to the others."

Piero smiled, and we got into the car and started up the road. We pulled off the road and started across the open field. The car was bouncing almost uncontrollably. We headed for the space between the last man and the man in the red cap. He stopped and pulled a gun and began firing at us. Piero turned the car hard left, then hard right, and finally turned into him, hitting him with the car. We stopped and quickly disarmed him and threw him in the car and took off. He was in a lot of pain. Piero looked over to me for an opinion.

"Broken leg, maybe a broken hip," I said.

The gunshots drew the attention of the Carabinieri. There was a car with officers headed out to the road from the house.

We got back to the road just ahead of the men heading for a car. Piero took out a gun and shot out two of the tires. As we sped down the road, I looked out the back window. The Carabinieri at the house had four or maybe five men face down on the ground and other Carabinieri, they were arresting the others at the disabled car.

Piero asked, "What now?"

I was thinking, then responded, "Let's get the others. Then you will take one car and two of your men and our captive to someplace to question. I will take my car one way, and the others need to go separate ways. I'm sure the FBI is tracking us from the air. You and I will communicate through Signor Moretti and the satellite phones."

Piero smiled. He understood and liked the plan.

On the way to the Café, I turned to Piero and said, "This one was on the phone. He must have been talking to Aashiq, telling him what was happening on the ground. He won't be missed for a few hours. Aashiq will first be concerned, then think maybe he lost his phone. Then he will go underground. My guess is we have maybe two hours to get any information that will be useful. You take him someplace and see if you can get the location of Aashiq. I will take his phone and see if I can locate the phone he called with my resources."

I fired up the satellite phone and called Jim at the FBI.

"What's happened, Warren."

"Knock off the bullshit, Jim, you are watching from a drone in real-time. Listen, we don't have much time. I have a phone I took from a captive, who I think was on the phone with Aashiq at the time we captured him. How can we locate the other phone on the call?"

"Turn it on and see if it's password protected."

" I did, and it came on; no password needed."

"Good, it was a burner phone, leave it on we will access it and get the last number called and the location. Burners are great for keeping us from knowing who is using it, but other than that, if we get ahold of one, we can tell all the calls made. Good job, Warren."

I hung up just as we were getting to the café. I got out and told Piero I would go back to my room and await his call.

Driving back to my room, I started thinking, the FBI was watching every move yesterday. They allowed Moretti's men to capture those two terrorists. They knew Moretti's men would torture them to death. If they had stepped in and arrested them, they would not be able to. The days of whisking them off to a black base were over for a time. That was why Jim wanted the Moretti family involved. It was never for their street connections.

I entered my room and laid on the bed, and thought, "Would the FBI have allowed those two last night to capture and torture me? If they had a drone up, wouldn't the FBI had seen Aashiq leaving the scene? Would they not have followed him.?" It is sad to trust a crime family more than the FBI.

Just then my satellite phone started to vibrate, I answered it. It was from Jim Marino.

"Warren, are you there?"

"Yes. It's me, Jim."

"I have the information you asked for on that person you sent me. He is associated with a group called *Allah's Army*. He is related to the leader who has a brother. What kind of mess do you have yourself in this time? Do you need me to send someone to give you a hand?"

"No, Jim, I think the problem is almost over. Are you coming to the baptism?"

"I wasn't asked."

"You are being asked now. Your godson is the godfather; I would love to have you as my guest. I will give you the inside scoop then."

"Send me the dates, and I will clear my calendar."

"Thanks, Jim."

I hung up and laid back down; with most of the terrorists caught and Aashiq soon to be, I could relax. Then my personal phone started to vibrate.

"Hello?"

"Warren, it's Maria, Can you talk?"

"Yes. It's great to hear your voice."

Chapter 25

"I WILL BE COMING home this weekend; are you free? Maybe we can spend some time together?"

"I will be finished soon and would enjoy spending the weekend with you." I will be driving back to my rented apartment in Florence tomorrow. Give me a call when you arrive. Think about what you would like to do; I am up for anything. How is your father?"

"He's a lot better now; they have gotten his blood pressure under control. They adjusted his medication. Thanks for asking. See you on Saturday."

I laid back down on the bed, focusing my thoughts on Maria. "Before this goes any farther, I have to be honest with her about not wanting any more children or being married again." Then thought again of the quote by Raymond Chandler. "There is no trap so deadly as the trap you set for yourself." I closed my eyes and fell asleep.

The next morning, I arose with the sunlight. I decided to stop by Lucca and to thank Catherina for her help and to let her know everything is OK, and she didn't have to look over her shoulder anymore. I picked up my phone and called her.

"Pronto"

"Catherina, it's Warren."

"Are you OK. . . . Is everything OK?"

"I'm fine, and everything is done and finished. I'm driving back to Florence today and would like to meet you for coffee this morning on my way through Lucca."

"That would be great! You will not believe what happened. The man I was negotiating with called me and said after some thought he would let me rent the space. Do you remember it? In the piazza across from where we ate. I can meet you there; I am there now, making it ready. I would love to show you."

"I'm leaving now. A presto."

I arrived at the shop and walked in. Catherina was in jeans and a red plaid shirt with her hair covered in a scarf. She was handling a mop like a crazy person. She looked up and smiled with great excitement. "Warren, come in, I want to show you my ideas for the place."

She showed which wall would have paintings, and in what area she would have sculptures and how she would arrange the lighting. It was fun to see her so excited.

When we were finished, we started to the restaurant across the piazza. As Catherina was locking up, her landlord next door was arranging some pots near his front door. He looked up, and she gave him a smile and nod: I did the same.

We were seated at a table outside, and we ordered two espressos and a torta to share.

"Catherina, I want to thank you for all your help. Because of your help, my business came to a quick conclusion."

"It was nothing, Warren."

I smiled. "You knew you were putting yourself at risk."

"Not really, Warren. I knew you would protect me. I am glad it all worked out."

Our coffees came; she took a sip, and as she was setting her coffee down, she said, "I am curious as to why the change of heart with my landlord. When he called me, at first, I refused to talk to him. As I told you, I was sure his demands were too high, but he insisted I listen to him. I told him I had changed my mind about the place. He begged me to take it. He even lowered the amount of the rent." Just then, she looked up, looking for my tell.

I was waiting for it and had composed a very confused look on my face and responded, "Did he give a reason?"

She smiled. "He said his sales have been down, and after thinking about it, the foot traffic to the gallery would be good for his business."

"Well, there, you have the answer."

We finished our coffees, and I promised I would attend the Grand Opening of the gallery, and I left for Florence.

Halfway to Florence, my satellite phone began to vibrate.

"Pronto"

"Signor, Steelgrave, it's, Piero; we have Aashiq. Do you want to come to where we have him?"

"No. Find out what's left of the cell, bank account numbers, associates, and supporters. Tell Signor Moretti we need to meet."

"OK."

I arrived at my rented apartment in Florence, about 4:00 in the afternoon. To no surprise, two FBI agents were there to greet me as I got to my front door: Jim Dempsey and John Ramsey.

"Come in fellows, have a seat. Coffee?"

"No. We won't be that long."

Jim didn't look pleased. In fact, he was pissed. I set down my backpack, reached in, taking out the protocol, and set the folder on the table.

"The protocol?"

"Yes, Jim, the protocol."

Jim's mood lifted a little, but not much.

"Where is Aashiq, Warren?"

"I thought you would have him by now."

"Moretti has him, and the FBI wants him."

"So why tell me. Go ask Moretti." Then I got mad. "Were you going to let Aashiq's men capture me in that alley?"

Jim looked down at his feet, sheepishly, and said, "No. We could tell you weren't in any real danger?"

"Sure, you could. If it weren't for Moretti's man Piero, I would probably be dead, and Aashiq would have the protocol. They were in my waistband at the time."

"Sorry, Warren. We made a mistake."

"Sorry, my ass. You made a calculated risk."

Jim shrugged his shoulders. "We still need Aashiq."

"Sorry. I can't help you. I did my part now I am done."

Jim stood up to leave. He stopped at the door and turned and held up the folder with the protocol and said, "Thank you for this and for not letting Signor Moretti get them. The world owes you a debt of gratitude." Then he and John Ramsey left.

My phone started vibrating. It was Piero.

"Pronto."

"Signor, Steelgrave, Signor Moretti would like to meet at the Ristorante Galleria in Milan tomorrow?"

"OK. Say 11:30 a.m."

"That will be fine."

Chapter 26

HE LOOKED UP out of the small trench he was laying in to see the rest of his group being arrested. He was the only one not captured or killed. He lay there until dark, and when he was sure it was safe to get up and leave. He knew what to do. He would steal the first car he came across and make his way to the safe house near Lucca and meet up with Aashiq and the rest of any survivors.

When he got to the safe house, the FBI was there. He watched from behind a tree as the FBI was taking Aashiq and two others into custody. Suddenly, the two men attacked their guard, and Aashiq took off running. He made it to the road when a car pulled up. Two men got out and grabbed Aashiq, and they got into a car and drove away. He wasn't the only one watching what was happening.

He was alone with no money or passport, stuck in Italy. He sat down, depressed, wondering if he would ever see his wife and two daughters again. He was not a true believer in the cause but joined Aashiq's group as a way to protect his family. Life was very hard for him and his family. He had better join Isis, or his wife and daughters would be brutalized, raped, and killed. Aashiq's group seemed a better choice. The family would be protected and given a small income; Aashiq's group would not see any fighting. They were a small group of hackers; their war was electronic. It gave him the best chance to return someday to be with his family. Now, what to do. Then he remembered the hidden cash. It was hidden in the hollow of a tree in the back of the property. It was put there for this type of emergency.

When he was sure they were all gone, and it was safe, he made his way to the tree, hoping the money was still there. It was. Five thousand euros. He took it and headed to Lucca, where he could buy a prepaid cell phone.

Having purchased a phone, he called the only person he knew could help.

"Hello."

"Bahir, it's Abir, the group has been taken down. I'm the only one left.

Bahir was shocked. "The whole group? Aashiq, him too?

"Yes. I watched as Aashiq was driven off by the Moretti family."

"I will make some calls. I will call you back at this number with what you are to do next."

Abir walked to a coffee bar to have a coffee and wait. Soon Abir's phone pinged. It was a text message that contained a name, Mohamed, and an address with instructions to follow. He finished his coffee and started off to the address.

He took a taxi to the address in the text. It was an apartment on the other side of Lucca. He knocked on the door, and a man opened the door.

"I am Abir. I was told to meet Mohamed at this address."

The man motioned him to come in. He entered the apartment and was asked to sit at a table in the small kitchen. In just a few moments, a man entered the kitchen and sat down at the table across from Abir.

"Welcome, my brother. I am Mohamed. I have been asked to debrief you. After, you will stay here until it is decided what to do with you."

The debriefing was more like an interrogation. It was clear Mohamed was concerned he might be undercover for the FBI. How did the FBI know about the safe house, and why was he the only one to get away? He was not going home to see his wife; that was for sure. He would have to prove his loyalty first if they decided not to kill him.

Mohamed finished the debriefing and asked if he would like something to eat. Abir was not hungry but was tired. He was taken to a spare bedroom to rest. Lying in the dark, Abir had visions of being asked to wear a suicide vest to prove his loyalty. He still had the money from the tree. If he ran, they would kill his wife and children. He lay there, thinking through all his options. His best bet was to wait and see what choices God would present him. He closed his eyes and started a deep prayer.

Abir was more tired than he had thought. During his prayer, he slipped into a deep sleep. He slept through the whole afternoon and through the night. When he woke up and ventured out of the bedroom, Mohamed was sitting at the kitchen table. He was drinking a coffee and fondling a packet.

"Abir, good morning, have a seat and something to eat, and a coffee. There are cheeses and fruit."

Abir sat and started eating while Mohamed made him an espresso. Mohamed set the coffee on the table near Abir and sat opposite him. Sliding the packet over to Abir, he said, "This is a passport and plane ticket for you to go home. Aashiq's brother wants you home for more debriefing."

Abir thought, "They must be planning something and don't want me around until they know I'm not undercover."

Abir took the packet and asked, "When do I leave?"

"Tonight."

Aashiq's brother, Miksa, felt Abir had to be an FBI informant. It was too convenient; the FBI finding the house, and Abir getting away. He would get to the bottom of this. Someone had to pay for his brother's capture or death.

Abir knew what was in store for him when he arrived home. While waiting to board the plane, he started to form a plan. He had information the FBI could use and enough money to bribe his way to safety. The trick was to take his family with him.

Abir landed in Tehran. When he got off the plane, two men were waiting to take him to their group's headquarters. He would wait until they crossed through the border and into Iraq before attempting an escape. The village where his wife and children are was in Iraq near the border; with some luck, that is where they would cross. Looking out the window, it was late afternoon: it would be dark in a couple of hours.

They had crossed the border, and it was almost dark. Abir could feel the tension rise in the vehicle. Then he saw the silhouette of a small village against the last red sliver of sunset: his village. They slowed down to take a dirt road. When they started to turn onto the road, he made his move and jumped out of the car. He started running as hard as he could towards the village and his home, praying his family was there.

Without knocking, he burst into the small hut of a house. His wife and daughters looked up, shocked, and frightened. Then his wife ran to him and throwing her arms around him and crying said, "Abir, it's you . . . it's really you."

"Quickly, we must leave now, take nothing."

As they left the house, Abir's wife asked, "Where are we going?"

"We must make our way to the Americans sector before we get caught."

She stopped . . . "We are in the American sector. They took over this area last week."

Abir looked down the street and saw an American patrol coming. He looked to the heavens and whispered, *"Thank you."*

Chapter 27

O N MY WAY to have lunch with Signor Moretti, my thoughts turned to Maria and the upcoming Baptism. I will tie up any loose ends at lunch today with Signor Moretti, then a long relaxing weekend with Maria. God, it felt good not to be running for my life.

I found a space to park at the minus three-level in a garage close to the Galleria. I took the stairs up the three levels to the street and walked the short distance to the Galleria. I walked into the Galleria and straight to the restaurant and introduced myself to the head waiter. He quickly took me through the restaurant to the dining room in the rear of the restaurant.

Gino was sitting near the door, and Signor Moretti was sitting at the far end of the table with a glass of wine. I walked in and turning to Gino said, "Ciao, Gino."

His only response was an annoyed glance in my direction before returning to his guard position. Signor Moretti stood, and with an outstretched hand, motioned me to take the seat to his left. Out of nowhere, a waiter appeared to take my drink order and present the day's specials. I ordered a red wine and the risotto with zucchini flowers.

On the table was a file. After the waiter left, Signor Moretti slid it over to me.

"Signor Steelgrave, here is information we got from Aashiq. Bank accounts, list of those who helped fund his organization, and a summary of his . . . interrogation."

"How much money was in the bank accounts?" Signor Moretti kind of rolled his eyes and responded with a smirk.

"Nothing." He continued, "The family wants to thank you. We have Mauro back. The FBI called, he is alive and just coming out of a coma, too soon to tell if he will make a complete recovery, but still, it was a great surprise, and the family is grateful."

Our lunch came, and we discussed the author, Raymond Chandler, throughout lunch.

I left the restaurant, and on the way to my car, I called Jim Dempsey.

"What's up, Warren?"

"I have received a file from Signor Moretti for you. I am returning tonight. When can we meet, and I give it to you?"

"How about I come by tomorrow, say 9:00?"

"Good. I will see you tomorrow."

I was just putting on the coffee and setting out a plate with some fruit and some pastries when the bell rang. I looked at my watch: the FBI is never late. I buzzed him in and waited for him at the door.

"Ciao, Warren. Buongiorno."

"Buongiorno. Come in, the coffee is just ready."

Jim came in and sat at the table as I was pouring two espressos. I set the coffees down and slid over to Jim the file I had received from Signor Moretti minus the summary. As Jim started looking through the file, I gave a summary of what it contained.

"I see there is no money in any of the bank accounts."

"What did you expect, Jim. You had to know once Signor Moretti was involved, he would take all he could. I thought it generous he gave you the information in the file without asking a fee. He did want me to express the family's appreciation for saving Mauro."

Jim just gave a small smile. Jim could tell I was still upset about what happened in the alley that other night. He started to apologize again, but I stopped him. It was the second time he left me hanging. We have a strange relationship. We respect each other but don't really trust each other. Two years ago, it was the Moretti family chasing me. They wanted to kill me and a friend over the Tesla files I had recovered. I called Jim, who was searching for my friend Tom as a missing person. I called Jim and told him I had Tom with me and wanted to turn him in until I could post the files online. Jim wanted information I wouldn't give him and said no. With Tom not missing anymore, the FBI had no more involvement. Then two weeks later, one of his agents saved my life at my daughter's wedding. But only because he was afraid of losing the Tesla files.

Jim finished his coffee and stood to leave. I walked him to the door, and he turned and said, "The FBI thanks you for what you did. You did a great service for your country."

"You said that the other day, Jim."

He smiled, extending his hand, and we shook, and he left.

I checked the time, it was 10:00; I will call Maria.

"Pronto."

"Ciao, Maria. It's Warren. I have a moment and thought I would call. Is it a bad time?"

"No, Warren, I was just going to call you. Is everything OK?"

"Yes, everything is finished. What time shall I pick you up on Saturday morning, 9:00?"

"Yes. I will see you Saturday, Warren."

Chapter 28

MIKSA WAS PACING back and forth, waiting to be given a briefing on how it was that Abir escaped. "Maybe I have more traitors among us," he thought.

Azhar, Miksa's most trusted lieutenant, walked into the room. They grew up together and were the same age. Azhar was a true believer in the cause, and like Miksa, he was worried too.

"Well, Azhar, what do those two fools have to say for themselves?"

Azhar explained in detail what had happened and how Abir managed to escape. Azhar went into great detail as to why he believed them.

"I know them both and their family's; they are good and loyal soldiers, Miksa."

"How did this happen? Are you saying this Abir was that smart he destroyed the complete cell and now I have heard that my brother was killed in the raid! Someone has to pay; pay in a way it sets an example."

"My first information is that Aashiq kidnaped a member of the Moretti family. Their informants on the street gave information to the FBI to help track the cell."

"A mob family working with the FBI! There must be more to this Azhar."

"I'm still checking. I will have more in a day or two."

They said their goodbyes, and both put on burqas before leaving. Damn these American drones; always overhead somewhere. They flew so high you could not hear or see them. Their ever-present threat was terrible stress on you.

***

I got to Maria's apartment just before 9:00 on Saturday morning. She must have been watching for me out her window; just as I got to the main door, it buzzed and unlocked before I could ring her apartment. I went in, and she was already coming down the stairs with a picnic basket and a blanket under her arm. At the bottom of the stairs, she handed me the basket and freeing her arms to give me a hug and kiss. Then she said, "Warren, I want to take you to another park. It's going to be hot today, and this park is covered with trees and mostly shade. It always has a cool breeze coming from the Arno. I want you to tell me all that happened while I was gone; don't leave out any detail."

With that, we were off. The park was quite a distance. It was as she said, totally in the shade a few blocks from the Arno, and very deserted. We spread out the blanket and sat down, opened a bottle of wine, and I began my story. Of course, I left out any mention of Catherina and how close I was to being caught.

"Warren, tell me about the baptism. Is everything all set?"

"Not really. I have been a little busy. My cousin in the village has places to stay for everyone, and the church notified. I will go back tomorrow and finish the details with the food. We will have a reception at the restaurant after the ceremony. Can you come with me?"

"No. I have a few things I have to take care of here. I will come the following week."

"Take the train, Maria, and I will pick you up."

She agreed and pushed me back onto the blanket and began kissing me. Not happy with my response, she sat up and asked, "What's wrong, Warren?"

I sat up and stared out across the park, searching for the right words. I felt before this went any further; she had to understand my feeling about having more children.

"Maria, I am not sure what you . . ." Struggling for the right words I went on. "What I'm trying to say is because of our age difference . . . I mean, because of my age you need to understand I don't want to have another family. I care for you a lot. You're young, and I am sure you want to have children." I glanced over to check on her reaction. She had a large smile on her face and was shaking her head a little from left to right.

"Oh, Warren, why so serious? Some years back, I was pregnant and had complications. I lost the baby and almost my life. The doctor said it was too dangerous for me to ever get pregnant again and tied my tubes. I am sorry, I assumed you did not want more children. It has ended a lot of my relationships. Most men want a family. I am lucky I have a niece and a nephew; I get to spoil. If we are baring our souls, it's my turn. . . . I love you and enjoy being with you, but I will not commit my life to someone who's heart is somewhere else. I will not have you hold me in your arms and have you thinking of someone else."

She turned to me and waited for my response. I was searching for the right words.

"Well, Maria, I am glad we cleared the air. I understand and would not expect you to. Thank you for your directness." With a slight smile, I continued, "Being honest is a good start to any relationship, don't you think? I am ready to see where this one goes."

She smiled and pushed me down on the blanket and started kissing me. I laid there with her in my arms, totally content.

***

Miksa was sitting at the table in his small house when Azhar walked in and sat down across from Miksa.

"How close are the Americans, Azhar?"

"Very close, they will take over this sector in a few hours. We need to leave soon."

Miksa nodded, he understood then said, "Have you heard anything more about what happened to my brother's cell?"

Azhar was hoping to avoid the subject. He knew how close Miksa was to his brother and didn't want emotions to cloud Miksa's judgment, especially now with the American backed forces so close. It was going to be tough enough to get out. Miksa looked straight into Azhar's eyes and said, "Tell me what you know, Azhar."

Azhar thought, "How much do I tell him." Then said, "What I have been told is Aashiq's men had tortured Mauro Moretti and had gotten the information for the hiding place of the protocol. They left him for dead as the FBI was closing in. Later they found out the information they got was incorrect and that Mauro might be in FBI custody and still alive. Mauro was the nephew of a very powerful Mafia leader who had heard the same rumors. What happens next is unclear, but it appears both groups worked together to find the cell. The enemy of my enemy is my friend. They used a Warren Steelgrave to search for the hidden protocol. I think they set a trap with Steelgrave as the bait, and Aashiq took it. Following Steelgrave led the FBI straight to the cell. How much is true, I don't know; it's not important. We must leave now if we are to avoid capture and live to fight another day."

"Not important to you," Miksa thought. He was not your only family member left. They left and headed to the border of Iran.

Chapter 29

I WAS APPROACHING THE village at just about sunset and thinking of Maria. I ended up checking out of the rented apartment and staying with Maria for the extra days. I have ten days to get the house in shape, and the arrangements all set for the baptism. I was feeling good about my relationship with Maria. I somehow felt differently about Cindy. I haven't thought about her, in the same way, the last few days. I would be damned if I would let a woman, I wasn't with have control of my life.

I walked into the house and started for the bar; I haven't had a martini in weeks. Then I stopped and thought, "No drinking until after the baptism. You need to be clear in your thinking to sort out your emotions."

I grabbed a cigar and headed out to the terrace to enjoy some jazz and the rest of the sunset. Just as I sat down, the phone rang: it's Stephanie.

"Hello, Dad. Do you have a moment?"

"Sure, Steph. What's up?"

"Just checking in. Any last-minute details I should be concerned about. I don't want to offend anyone because I do something culturally inappropriate."

"Nothing to worry about. How many people and how much luggage will you have, so I know how many cars to bring to pick you up?"

"You don't have to worry about picking us all up. We have rented a Jeep for the week. Jim and Cindy want to go to Florence for a few days after the baptism. Maybe you could join us?"

"Not possible. I have a friend who is staying the week, and I promised to show her around Piemonte. How's the baby?"

"She is fine; starting to walk. That's about it, looking forward to seeing you. Love you, Dad."

"Love you too, Steph."

After ending the call, I sat there in the calm of the evening finishing my cigar. Watching the smoke slowly rise, I thought, "Just what I would love to do; spend a few days with Cindy and her husband and Maria in Florence."

On Thursday, everyone started arriving. First to arrive was my son John and his family. I went to pick them up while Maria made a small lunch for when we returned. After lunch, it was time to pick up Sherry and her family. It was about 8:00 in the evening when Stephanie and her group arrived. I had excused myself to go upstairs for a moment when I heard the commotion downstairs. As I came down the stairs into the living room, everyone was talking and introducing themselves to Maria.

Standing at the bottom of the stairs, I saw her. She was standing near the bar by herself when she looked up, and our eyes met. Now I know how an alcoholic feels when he has been on the wagon a few years and hasn't thought of a drink. Then he walks out onto a friend's terrace to admire the sunset, and they are serving martinis. Not vodka martinis, ice-cold gin martinis . . . with jazz playing softly. The lyrics of a song by Vince Gill came to mind. A song he wrote about his feelings for Amy Grant, *Whenever You Come Around*. Just then, I felt an arm around my waist. It was from Maria.

"Warren, is that Cindy standing by the bar?"

"What? . . . Oh, yes, it is."

With that, she let go and started over to Cindy with me following. Reaching Cindy, she extended her hand.

"Cindy O'Brian? I am Maria Sategna, It is so good to finally meet you; our paths have crossed in the past. I feel as if I know you because of Warren's books. I helped with your escape from Florence, which was the first book, and I was Maria in the second book."

"It is good to meet you, Maria, and thank you for your past help."

"I have bought your latest album and play it all the time."

"Thank You."

Looking around the room, Maria asked, "Which one is your husband?"

"He didn't come. He had a planned fishing trip with our sons."

I felt stupid, not knowing what to say when Sherry walked up, handing Cindy and Maria a glass of wine and saying to me, "What, Dad, no martini?"

I smiled, and putting my arm around Maria's waist said, "I have given up drinking for a while. Thought I would give the liver a rest."

I can always count on Sherry to save me whenever she's around. Then Maria took Cindy by the arm and said, "Come with me, Cindy, let's go upstairs and out on the terrace. I have a million questions to ask you," as they headed upstairs, I heard Maria asking about Cindy's upcoming concert dates.

"Come on, Dad, show me the rest of the house."

After I thought everyone had left and Sherry's family went to bed, I looked in my bedroom, and Maria was fast asleep. I went downstairs and poured myself a glass of what was left of the iced tea and went out on the terrace to think. Cindy was sitting in what used to be her chair. I walked over and sat in what has always been my chair. "I thought you had left with Stephanie, Cindy?"

"I told them to leave the door unlocked that I wanted to spend some time alone walking through the village. God, how I missed this house and sitting out here with you."

I didn't know how to respond, so I didn't. After a time, Cindy went on.

"Maria seems very nice and has such a commanding presence."

I wanted to change the subject from Maria and leave her out of this conversation.

"How are things at home, Cindy?"

"That's the Warren I know direct and straight to the point. We are struggling through a loveless relationship. We never remarried, which is a good thing. He is more mistrusting then ever and hates my career. For me, my career has been my savior. Keeps me busy, and I take my son with me on summer tours, which helps with my husband's insecurities; all in all, it's not too bad a life until my son leaves home, and you?"

"I just finished another book that will be published this summer. Spending a lot of time doing some introspective work on myself," Cindy interrupted.

"Ah. That's why you weren't drinking tonight."

I smiled and continued, "Yeah. I am trying to work out some emotional issues, and I'm a firm believer that cannot be done drinking an average of four martinis a day."

"Warren . . . How serious is it with Maria?"

I hesitated, trying to come up with the right words. "I think it could be a lot more than what it is. The problem is me. I don't want to involve anyone in my life until I have worked out those emotional issues and have a handle on why so much drama. I am tired of living a life with so much drama. It always seems to end badly . . . worse for those closest to me."

Before she could say anything, I stood up and said, "It's getting late, Cindy. I'm going to bed. It is good seeing you. See you in the morning."

She nodded, and I left. As I started for the stairs, I caught a glimpse of Maria's robe going up the stairs. When I got up the stairs and entered the bedroom, Maria was in bed with her back to the door. I undressed and got into bed. Just as I got settled, Maria reached over and took my hand. I fell asleep thinking, "Maria must have come downstairs for a drink of water. I wonder how much of my conversation with Cindy she heard."

Chapter 30

"WHAT DO YOU think, Jeff?"

Jeff was studying the FBI report he had just received. Leaning back in his chair and nodding his head slightly and thinking, he answered, "Well, John, something just isn't right. The FBI says they got all the terrorists in that cell, but, Abir knows too much detail of what happened to have not been there." I think he is telling the truth, and if what he has given us so far is verified, he could turn out to be a great assist."

John wasn't so sure. He and Jeff had been interrogating terrorists for about four years and never has one turned himself over and wanted to change sides.

"I don't know, Jeff. I think he might be a plant, you know, a double agent."

"Maybe, we will know in a few days when we find out if what he has given us is verified. It would be a great win for our side."

"Do you think if he were a plant, he would give us the information we couldn't verify?"

"I'm not saying you're wrong, John. Let's play along and see what he keeps giving us, and we will have to be careful about what he has access to. In time we will know. It could make a big difference if we had someone who could decipher intercepted messages in real-time, and not have to wait a day or two. It could mean stopping an attack instead of being a day late."

After a few days, word came the information so far was verified. It was decided Abir and his family would be moved to Virginia and away from the daily operations going on in the Middle East. He would work within the intelligence community where they could keep surveillance on him.

***

Miksa and Azhar made it across the border by blending in with refugees fleeing the violence of the approaching collation forces led by the Americans. There they met with others of their group to begin reorganizing the plan to attack the United States infrastructure using cyberspace. If they had received the protocol, they would have already taken down a lot of the command and control of the coalition forces. Still, they had learned a lot; soon, they would be ready to attack some of the weaker systems like banking and some power grids. Those systems are vulnerable to hacking. Abir would be missed; he was leading the effort and the best hacker they had. The setback was only temporary.

***

Jim Dempsey was running a little late as he drove to the secret facility, which was where Abir was being held. The FBI wanted Jim to interview Abir. Jim was involved with the takedown of the terrorist cell outside Lucca, and the FBI wanted his assessment of Abir firsthand. As he was parking the car, he thought of Warren and how instrumental he was in bringing down the cell. At least it was resolved before the baptism, which was this weekend.

Jim walked into the building, showed his badge to the receptionist and guard, and took the elevator to the third floor. Walking into room 324, he saw a man perhaps forty years old sitting at a small table. Jim walked over and sat across from the man, not saying a word. They both sat there in silence. Jim wanted to see if he could provoke some emotion, maybe some nervousness: nothing. Jim could not detect any suppressed anger or resentment, only calmness and serenity. Jim finally spoke, "Good morning, Abir, my name is Jim Dempsey. I was involved in taking out your cell and killing your friends." Still no hostility. "Tell me your story starting with why you became a terrorist."

Abir started at the beginning and how he never wanted to hurt or kill anyone. How all his choices were made to keep his family safe. He explained the threat to his family if he didn't cooperate with Isis. After about ninety minutes, he was finished with his story, and Jim asked, "Tell me, Abir, why do you want to help us?"

"To protect my family. So my children can grow up with choices different than I had."

"How far along was your group with the plan to take down major institutions and infrastructures?"

"Not very far. Unlike the West, our culture stifles science and independent thought. It is very hard to solve a problem creatively when you have been raised how to think. You first must retrain your thinking. You are not looking for the answer; you must create the answer. That is why the work Mauro Moretti was doing was so important. The protocol he was developing had the answers to find a kind of road map to defeat firewalls."

Jim was shaking his head slightly. It was making sense to him.

"Abir, did you ever meet, Mauro Moretti?"

"Yes, I was there when they brought him to the farmhouse. They put him in a room with me guarding him. He was very scared. We talked for a while. He knew the importance of what he had developed and was sure they would never find it. If they did, they wouldn't understand how to use it. I told him I was a fan of the great Tesla. His mood changed a bit. He was surprised I knew who Tesla was, and we started talking about the great man. He was a great fan of Tesla and the way Tesla protected his work, not trusting anyone. That's when I knew the protocol was written in code. Tesla and Leonardo DaVinci both wrote a lot of their notes in code. In the short time we had together, it was clear this was a very intelligent man. His thinking process was like no one I ever met."

"So why did they kill him, Abir?"

"I pleaded with them to spare his life. They have no respect for a man like Mauro, he represented the West and all that they hate. When they thought they had the information they needed, they sent two men to go verify it was correct before killing him, but the FBI showed up.

Confident they had the information they killed him, and we all fled. It wasn't until the next day that they realized they had misunderstood something in his directions and could not find the protocol. Then they found out Mauro might be alive and in the custody of the FBI. If smart enough, they would get a second chance to retrieve the protocol. As it turned out, they weren't."

Jim, nodding his head slightly with raised eyebrows, and a small smirk acknowledged he understood. Taking out a file he brought with him, he said, "Abir, can you tell me about this?"

Handing Abir a file that included a document already decoded by the FBI as a test, Jim waited for Abir to respond. Abir read through the transcript that was in the file and said, "Mr. Dempsey, this is a correspondence between a commander and his field commander in charge. It is giving him the details for a car bombing of the American Embassy in Paris. It gives the details of how it is to take place . . . . do you want me to read all the details; it is to take place in two days!"

"No. Abir, I want you to transcribe it all into English. Here is a laptop to use, I will be back in an hour."

Jim left and took the elevator to the top floor and walked into the operation officer's office. It was a large corner office with one wall that was glass behind the large wooden antique desk. The office and everything in it were designed to intimidate and project the power of the director, Zac Nohr of the NSA. Zac was approaching sixty. Just under six feet in height, short gray hair, trim and fit in a gray suit and dark blue tie. All the gray highlighted his piercing hazel eyes. He was sitting at the desk. In a chair in front was Commander John Hutson. The commander was a tall man over six feet tall and was in uniform. The director stood from his chair, and Jim Dempsey addressed him.

"Good morning, Director... Commander Hutson, good to see you again, sir." Shaking both men's hands, he kept standing and went on. "I think he is on the square. I gave him a transcript of communication we intercepted and decoded two days ago and gave him a laptop to translate it into English. We have already stopped the plot. It took us most of a day to decode and understand what they were planning. Amir read it to me as if he was reading it in English. Now let's see if he tries to use the laptop to warn anyone we are onto the plan or changes some of the details. I think we can use him. We will keep him working on things we already know and things we intercept to keep checking his accuracy, and how well he can read and write English. The real test will come when we intercept something imminent and don't have the time to decipher it. If he can decode it in real-time and saves the day, he will be a great asset."

The director spoke first. "Sounds like a plan. Let's all hope this guy is for real."

Jim said his goodbyes and left.

Chapter 31

I AWOKE THE MORNING of the baptism and found that Maria was already up and downstairs. I lay in bed listening to the chatter downstairs and the clinking of dishes and glasses. The house was awake and buzzing with energy. I looked at my watch. It was 8:00, and the baptism was going to happen just before the 11:00 morning mass. I got up and headed for the shower while it wasn't being used. Maria never did mention anything about the other night. Maybe she never heard any of my conversation with Cindy.

In the shower, I became lost in emotion and how uncomfortable I was with the whole affair so far. Getting dressed, I heard Cindy's voice downstairs and wondered how uncomfortable she must be watching Maria make coffee in the same kitchen she was in command of not so long ago. We had such wonderful times in this house, and now another woman is making love and sleeping in that same bed we enjoyed. I looked again at my watch; I only have to get through the next twenty-four hours.

I walked into the kitchen and said good morning to those there and poured myself a cup of coffee and walked outside to the terrace and addressed those guests outside. My house was being used as a gathering place for everyone to meet until it was time to walk the three blocks to church. I sat down, and no sooner had I placed my coffee on the table, Stephanie came up and handed me the baby.

"Watch her for me, Dad, I want to finish changing."

I got comfortable with the baby, and as I was holding her, everything around me faded away; it was she and I. Looking down at her; she was staring straight into my eyes and smiling. "Well, Mary, I wonder what life has in store for you?"

She reached up and touched my beard. "Stick with me kid, we will get through this day together."

She chuckled; she knew exactly what I meant. We had made a connection.

The church bells started to ring the call to worship as we were leaving the house. Entering the church and making

our way to the front pews, I looked over at Stephanie and her husband, Jim. It occurred to me that 150 years ago, they would have been my great grandparents here to baptize my grandfather. We sat down, and they, along with the godparents, were called up to the altar for the baptism. I started to become overtaken by emotion. It was then I caught Stephanie looking at me as our eyes met, she gave me a little smile and a wink. Sometime when you least expect it your children surprise you. They have been paying attention. She knew how much this would mean to me, even if I didn't. What a great gift.

After church, we all walked up to the restaurant for lunch and celebration. Many of my local friends and cousins came; most brought cards and little gifts to mark the importance of the day. After most left, the rest of us headed down the street to my house. We weren't there very long when Stephanie walked up to me with a card in her hand.

"Dad, when we walked in, I noticed this card on the bar with Mary's name on it. I opened it, and there was this baptism card. It had four five-hundred-euro banknotes. No name, and I am sure it wasn't here when we left for church. Do you have any idea where this came from and from who?"

"I have no idea. Someone obviously wanted to stay anonymous."

She walked away, shaking her head. I knew where it came from, Signor Moretti. He would not let something as important as a baptism go without acknowledging it. He also has enough respect for the family to not taint our family by connecting it in any way to his.

The day was coming to an end, and people were leaving. Some were headed home in the morning; others were headed off to other parts of Italy. Maria said she was going for a walk with Sherry and her family. I made my way upstairs and out onto the upstairs terrace with a cigar and an Iced Tea. Cindy walked out and sat down. Looking out over the village, she started rubbing the arms of the chair slightly. Then said, "I figured I would find you sitting out here. I wanted to say goodbye." I smiled and nodded. She went on. "I have been nominated for a Grammy." She looked over at me for my reaction.

"That is great, Cindy, I always said it would happen."

"Do you remember the promise you asked me to make?"

"Yes. I asked you to promise you would get me tickets."

Nodding and with a large smile, she said, "I'll have two tickets for you when I receive my allotment."

"Thank you."

We sat there a few moments, neither one of us knew what to say. Cindy got up and said goodbye and left. What an emotional day. I felt drained.

I was finishing my cigar when I heard Maria and Sherry enter the living room downstairs. I got up and went down to join them.

I walked into the room and over to Maria. Putting my arm around her shoulders, I said, "Sherry, where are the rest of the family?"

"They are coming along, the girls stopped to play with a dog. I wish we could stay longer. The kids must get back to school, but Robert and I discussed it last night and decided to take you up on your offer to come back this summer when the girls are out of school."

The rest of the evening, we sat outside and talked, catching up on family gossip. It turned out to be a very lovely weekend without any of the drama I feared.

Chapter 32

THE NEXT MORNING after breakfast, I drove the family to the airport while Maria finished straightening up around the house. When I returned home, Maria had prepared a small lunch and was setting it out on the terrace when I walked in. I said to her as I followed her outside, "That looks wonderful, Maria." She smiled, and we sat down to eat.

"I was surprised with Cindy; she was nothing like I had imagined. I thought she would be more of a diva." I looked over at her with an inquisitive look. "You know what I mean more narcissistic and manipulating. She was none of that. I found myself drawn to her, and I liked her a lot."

I went back to drinking my coffee and trying to find the words to acknowledge what she said and change the subject at the same time when my phone rang. It was from Jim Dempsey. Saved by the bell. "She reminds me a lot of you." Holding up one finger, I continued. "I have to take this call.

"Hello, Jim."

"Hello, Warren, do you have a minute we can talk?"

Concerned and with caution, I answered, "Only a minute."

"How was the baptism? Did everything go, OK?"

"It was a great weekend, and thanks for the card and silver cross."

I sat there waiting for the other shoe to drop with all the anticipation of waiting for the dentist to stick you with a shot of Novocain.

"I am in the Torino office and was wondering if you had time to meet. Something has come up, and I don't want to talk about it on the phone."

Looking over to Maria, I answered. "Maybe dinner at the Tre Re?" Maria, with an inquisitive look, was shaking her head, OK.

"Good, I will see you tonight, say 7:30?"

"7:30."

I looked over at Maria, who was smiling.

"What Maria?"

"Nothing, Warren, let's go see something until dinner."

"I read that at Fort di Bard there is a great exhibit of Henri Cartier-Bresson photographs. We can tour the fort and exhibit, Maria?"

"I would like that, Warren. I have seen pictures of the fort and would love to see it. Let's clean up the dishes and go."

We got to the Tre Re right at 7:30 and walked in. Luciano smiled and greeted us. "Buonasera, Warren," and turned his attention to Maria.

"Buonasera, Luciano, may I present Maria Sategna."

"Piacere mio, your guest is already here, follow me, please."

We followed him through the restaurant to a secluded table in the back. Jim always arrives early so that we aren't seen entering together, and has us seated well away from everyone. As we approached the table, Jim stood as I introduced him to Maria. I could tell he was surprised I was not alone.

"Good evening, Jim, may I introduce Maria Sategna."

"My pleasure, Maria."

We all sat down, and then Jim put it together.

"Excuse me, Maria, but weren't you the girl who came to Warren's rescue in the middle of the night in Florence?"

"You are referring to the girl in the second book who made her apartment available for the main character and friend to hide after the FBI left them to be caught and killed by the crime family?"

Jim was taken aback a little and nodded, yes.

"Well, I would never be so presumptuous to assume I was a character in a bestselling novel." Then she looked him straight in the eyes and with a slight tilt of the head, smiled.

At that point, Jim realized why I wasn't alone and that anything said would not leave the room.

After we ordered dinner, Jim started,

"I called, Warren, because the bureau could use your help."

I raised a hand to stop him before he could go on.

"Jim, every time I get involved with the FBI, I get used as bait."

Now Jim interrupted and slightly angry said, "Let's be fair, Warren, the first time you set yourself up as bait to rescue your friend's son and this last time . . . Well, I have apologized for that, but let's not forget it was the FBI that saved your and Cindy's life at the wedding. I don't remember you refusing our help with the stalker!"

"OK, Jim, enough said. This last time has been eating at me because you had lost control of your superiors. I just needed to get it off my chest. What do you need?"

Jim first started out by explaining the plight of Abir and how he came to be in custody.

"You trust this guy, Jim?"

"More and more every day. But here is the problem. He says from the chatter they are planning something big in the next eight months. It entails using the internet to take out some vital systems, banking, power grid, etcetera. If we understood Mauro's protocol, we could start protecting these systems. Abir says Mauro was a big Tesla fan, and he is sure he wrote them in code. Our top people have been working on the material you gave me, and they think he is right. We could use your help in contacting, Mauro. We have tried and have had no response."

"You must realize, Jim, Signor Moretti is in a very delicate position. If he is seen as working with the FBI, it could get him killed."

"I do realize that. That is why I am here asking for your help. The bureau would like you to convince them about the importance of Mauro helping us. He was willing to before he was abducted. This is so important the FBI is willing to do almost anything for his help." His voice slowed downed, and his head started moving up and down slowly as he continued, "It could be a very important arrangement for his family."

I thought for a minute about what he was suggesting and asked, "Jim, are you saying the FBI would be willing to drop charges or stop ongoing investigations?"

"Warren, you know I will not publicly say that. What I am willing to commit to would be to help the family if possible. That would have to be discussed directly with them so we are clear what kind of problems they would like help with. We feel they owe you for helping get Mauro back and at least give you an audience and listen with an open mind. Our fear is they think the FBI is looking hard at them for all the missing money from the bank accounts, and that is why they are keeping us at a distance."

Just then, our dinner arrived. I sat there thinking through what was said.

"Jim, give me a few days to think it through. I will get back to you by the end of the week."

Chapter 33

A FTER DINNER AND on the way home, Maria turned to me in the car and asked,

"Warren, what are you going to do? I don't see how you can refuse. If something big happened and you hadn't even tried to stop it, how could you live with yourself?"

"Maria, tomorrow I will call Signor Moretti. I don't totally trust the FBI. Once I say yes, I'm totally committed. I learned a long time ago to know how deep the water is before you dive in headfirst. I want to talk to Signor Moretti and gather what information I can. This could be more about going after the Moretti family then terrorism."

Maria hadn't thought of that, Thinking it through, she nodded her head in agreement. The rest of the way home, nothing more was said.

The next morning was a beautiful clear morning. You could hear the birds and a dog barking in the distance. It was cool outside, so we slipped on sweatshirts and had our coffee and a pastry outside on the terrace. I started to mention the Grammys and that Cindy promised me two tickets then decided not to. The Grammys were nine months away; by then, I might not even want to go.

I got up and excused myself to go call Signor Moretti. I went inside and down to the lower terrace. Gino answered the phone.

"Pronto."

"Ciao, Gino, it's Warren Steelgrave. Is Signor Moretti available?" He didn't answer; after about thirty seconds, Signor Moretti spoke.

"Yes?"

"Signor Moretti, thank you for the generous baptism gift I promised my daughter I would call for her . . . Something else has come up, can we meet?"

There was a long pause, then he said, "Friday afternoon; here 1:30."

"Thank you."

He ended the call with no goodbye. I walked into the house, and Maria was just coming down the stairs heading to the kitchen with the breakfast dishes.

"How did it go, Warren?" When she didn't get an immediate answer, she set the dishes on the counter and turned to stare at me with an inquisitive look. I was still contemplating the call in my mind. Raising both eyebrows and a slight nod to the side of my head. I said, "We have a meeting at his house on Friday afternoon at 1:30."

"And!"

"And?"

"Yes, and what else, Warren? Something has you concerned about the call."

"He never takes my call. He always has Gino call me back. Gino didn't even ask what the call was, about, just put me through to Moretti. He was expecting the call."

The rest of the week, we relaxed. We would take a day trip up to Aosta and toured Fort Bard. Always being back by 5:00 in the afternoon for cocktails and a snack of cheese and salami. We would sit out on the top terrace. Her with a glass of wine and me with a glass of iced tea.

Friday, we left early for the meeting with Signor Moretti. We had an early lunch at the restaurant Galleria then on to the city of Cremona to meet with Signor Moretti. We pulled up to the front of the house, parked, got out, and walked to the front door and rang the doorbell. Gino answered the door and invited us in. Standing in the foyer, I looked to my left and saw Signor Moretti standing in the living room. Immediately, he started towards us with a very pleasant smile. "How unusual," I thought. Then he spoke, and it became clear.

"Maria, so good to see you. How is your father?"

"Doing better, thank you."

"And your mom and the rest of the family?"

"All good."

I was a little shocked. Maria never let on she knew the Moretti family.

"Maria, would you like a coffee while you wait for Mr. Steelgrave and me to conclude a little meeting. We won't be too long."

"Yes, thank you."

As Gino escorted Maria to the dining room, I followed Signor Moretti to the library.

"Can I get you something to drink? A coffee, maybe?"

"No, thank you."

We both sat down in two wing-back chairs across a small table from each other. We both sat there for a moment until I realized Signor Moretti was waiting for me to begin.

"Thank you for seeing me. I think you are aware the FBI has been trying to reach Mauro." I was watching him for a tell, nothing. I went on. "They asked that I reach out to you and explain why they need to talk to, Mauro. They came to realize the protocol they received is in code. They would like Mauro's help in understanding them. Their concern is that you think they want to come after the missing money from the terrorist's bank accounts. They wanted me to assure you that is not the case."

Signor Moretti sat there thinking, then finally spoke.

"The world thinks Mauro is dead. If he were to help, it would soon be known, he is alive, and he would be hunted again. The risk is too great for him and the family. Surely you understand."

"I do. I am only the messenger and want you to know it wasn't about the money. Let me say this. The FBI has intercepted messages and knows Isis is planning a very big attack next year. They believe it will have to do with hacking into and using part of the internet. Taking down banking or the power grid. Your nephew can help stop it. He tried to help before. I am sure there is a way he can help that will limit his exposure. They also wanted me to tell you if you help in this matter, they will take a different view of some of your nonviolent business ventures."

He sat there thinking through it all, then stood. As I stood, he reached out, and we shook hands.

"Thanks for making the trip, Mr. Steelgrave. I will talk it over with the family."

Maria and I got to the car and started for home. After a few minutes, I turned to her and said, "Maria, you never mentioned you knew Signor Moretti."

"You can't own the amount of property my dad owns without having had to deal with him. It's not anything you talk about. He can be a very violent man, and you would never want to cross him like harboring two individuals he is hunting."

I got the message, and nothing more was said about Signor Moretti.

The rest of the spring and summer life was great. I started a new book; Maria and I split our time between my place in Muriaglio and her apartment in Florence. My daughter and her family came for three weeks until the middle of August. It was the beginning of fall, and I could tell Maria was beginning to lose her patience with me. She wanted more than a convenient lover.

Chapter 34

MIKSA WAS HAVING a coffee at a café near the Eiffel tower in Paris when Azhar sat down. A waiter walked over, and he ordered a coffee. When the waiter walked away, Azhar looked over to Miksa, who was staring and waiting.

"I have our new documents and tickets for a flight to Los Angeles tonight at 8:00. Don't go back to the apartment; the authorities are watching it."

"I have packed everything I needed yesterday, Azhar, and have it over at Mohamed's apartment."

"Good. I will meet you at the airport at 6:30. We will be picked up at the John Wayne airport and taken to a house in Tustin, California, near Los Angeles. There we can finish the work."

"Are you sure, Azhar? It's already November. The Grammys are only three months away. Why aren't we further along?"

"Everything is fine, Miksa. We make inroads, then they block us out. Our strategy is working, don't worry. All our attempts have been toward big systems, banking, power grids, and national security systems. It diverts their attention away from our real target, the Grammys. We have people working as roadies and in the departments that are receiving equipment. All we have to do is kill the power for about three minutes as the bomb is going through security. It will be in a large case for instruments. Once through security, it will be stored under the main stage. Near the end of the show, it will be detonated by a cell phone. Think about it. Twenty million people watching worldwide."

"I heard rumors that the person who had, developed the protocol is alive and helping to harden our targets."

Azhar was concerned. He knew Miksa was still wanting to avenge his brother's death and wasn't sure where this conversation was headed.

"I have heard rumors, but that is all I have heard. We need to keep focused on the task at hand."

"Azhar, I am keeping focus. What if he is alive and helping the Americans harden the targets? Then there is the problem with Amir."

"Amir?"

"Yes, Amir. We do not know what happened to him. What if he was embedded into the cell by the FBI. How did they find the cell, and why only one survivor? If Amir was working with the FBI, he could be helping them now?"

Azhar thought for a moment. That would explain a lot of what was happening with the targets. Every-time they pick a target to hack the FBI gets to it and hardens it first.

"How would he ever find out the Grammys are the target, Miksa?"

"There was a person Aashiq had people following. What do you know about him?"

"Not much. At first, Aashiq thought he might lead them to the hidden protocol, but he wasn't sure. He was a writer; I didn't hear anymore."

"Let's find him and find out what he knows. You stay back and find this person. Mohamed will help you. It shouldn't take very long. If he is a writer, most of his information should be in the public record."

Azhar nodded, he understood. It did make sense to find this writer, but he also knew Miksa wanted to avenge his brother's death with the brutal death of someone. This writer would do. He left Miksa, and on his way to meet Mohamad, he took out his cell phone.

"Mohamed, it's Azhar, there has been a slight change of plans. I am on my way to your apartment. We will drop off Miksa's things at the airport, then we have a little job to do. Do you remember the writer Aashiq was following; research our database of emails and find his name. Find out where he lives, we need to pick him up."

Arriving at Mohamed's apartment, Azhar rang the bell and was let in by Mohamed.

"Did you find the information on the writer, Mohamed?"

"I did, and his name was in an email. A Warren Steelgrave, I looked him up; he lives in a small village in northern Italy. The village's name is Muriaglio. Do you want to take the train to Turin and rent a car? If we drive, it will take about nine hours from Paris."

Azhar thought for a few moments then responded. "We will take the small van and drive. That way, there will be no record of us renting anything. We will steal some license plates from a similar van once we are in Italy. Are these Miksa's suitcases?"

"Yes."

"Let's go and drop them off at the airport. Miksa is waiting."

They arrived at the airport and found Miksa waiting just inside the main entrance.

"Have you the name of the writer, Azhar?"

"Yes, Miksa. His name is Warren Steelgrave; we are leaving now to go pick him up."

"What's the plan, Azhar?"

"We will abduct him, find an abandoned structure somewhere, and torture him until we get the information we want. Then we will kill him and dispose of the body where it will be found to send a message. If the hacker Mauro is alive, what do you want us to do?"

"Pick him up."

Azhar nodded, he understood; he and Mohamed headed for Italy.

Chapter 35

I JUST GOT HOME from the dry cleaners when I saw the mail lady leaving the house. With the clothes in one hand, I took out the mail and headed upstairs. After hanging up the clothes, I sat at the kitchen table and went through the mail. I smiled. Among some bills was an invitation to a gallery opening: Catherina's gallery in Lucca. I took out my phone and called Maria.

"Pronto."

"Ciao, Maria. It's Warren. I am calling to see if you received an invitation to a gallery opening next weekend?"

"I did, but I leave for Paris for a meeting with my father's doctors."

"Is he doing worse?"

"No. The doctor just wants to run some tests and check my father out. I didn't know you knew Catherina."

I didn't want to lie, and I didn't want to say anything that would lead to a long explanation of how well I knew her.

"When I was in Lucca, I ate at a restaurant where she worked. She remembered me from that party you and I went to, and I had too much to drink."

"Oh," was her reply with a bit of an edge.

"Call me when you return from Paris, Maria, and I will come to Florence for a while. I miss you."

Her voice brightened.

"I will, Warren. It's been a few weeks. I miss you also."

I hung up the phone, and looking at the invitation, I thought, "I guess things are working out with Catherina's landlord."

Azhar and Mohamed arrived in Muriaglo early on Saturday morning. Driving past the house, there was no car in the parking space, and the house had no lights on inside and appeared empty. They both looked at each other, and Azhar spoke.

"Maybe he is sleeping in?"

"It's almost 8:30, Azhar. What do you think we should do?"

"Let's park and walk over to the coffee bar in the little piazza and have a coffee. We can see what happens in a little while."

After their coffee, they walked back to the house and found that a woman was parked in the little parking spot in front of the house. She was heading up the steps with cleaning supplies when Azhar approached her. From the bottom step, he called up to her.

"Excuse me, is Signor Steelgrave home."

"No, he left for Lucca."

"Do you know when he will return?"

"No. All I know is Signor Steelgrave called and said he was going to a friend's gallery opening in Lucca and asked if I would clean the house and do the laundry while he was gone."

Azhar thanked her and walked back to the car, where Mohamed was waiting. They got into the car and left.

Warren's cousin Gino was across the street and had observed part of the exchange. After they drove off, he crossed the street and waited at the bottom of the stairs for Dominica to return for more supplies.

"Dominica, who were those men?"

"I don't know; they were looking for Warren."

"Did you ask them why?"

"No."

"I have told you in the past, when asked a question about someone by a stranger, answer with a question. Is Warren home? Who is asking? Does Warren live here? Why are you asking? Etcetera."

Dominica headed back up the stairs as Gino took out his phone. Gino sent Warren a text letting him know two strangers were in the village looking for him.

I was just entering my room when my phone buzzed. It was a text from Gino. "Who would be looking for me," I thought.

***

"How long before we get to Lucca, Mohamed?"

"We should be there in four hours. I have someone we can stay with. Once there, we can get on Facebook and check for events this weekend. Without too much difficulty, we should find the gallery opening event."

Mohamed, who was driving, glanced over at Azhar, who was nodding slightly and focused. Arriving at the friends in Lucca, Mohamed got on the computer and quickly found an event for a gallery opening that night starting at 7:00.

***

My hotel was only a few blocks from the gallery. It was still three hours before the start of the event. With nothing to do, I decided to walk over and take a look. When I got there, Catherina was finishing up details. When I walked in, she looked up and gave me a big smile. Walking over to me, she stopped just in front, and with both hands on her hips, said, "Warren, why didn't you call. I wasn't sure you received the invitation; you might have been traveling."

"I wanted to surprise you."

Giving me the biggest hug, she whispered in my ear, "Thank you."

Looking around, I said, "It looks great, Catherina. Things work out with the landlord?"

"Things are great with him." Then a long pause.

I stopped walking and turned to her to see why. Looking straight at me and focused looking for a tell, she went on.

"He said the strangest thing to me yesterday. He came over for a look and complimented me on the quality of the pieces in the gallery. Then asked if I would be sure to tell my friends how the gallery increased foot traffic in his store." Her focus on me increased as she went on. "I thought what a strange thing to say. It felt like he was sending a message to someone."

I didn't know how to respond, so I didn't; just shrugged my shoulders, indicating it seemed OK to me.

"Warren, I have a few errands to run before the opening, do you mind?"

"No, I was just stopping by for a moment. I will see you later."

I walked out of the gallery and stood on the sidewalk, looking around. Gino's text had put me on edge. Seeing nothing suspicious, I started walking to my hotel. Seeing Catherina jogged my memory, and I began thinking of the past events. Then it occurred to me I had never heard from Signor Moretti. I wondered if he ever contacted the FBI and if Mauro is working with them.

Sitting across the street watching the gallery, drinking coffees were Azhar and Mohamed.

"Let's go, Mohamed, maybe we will have the opportunity to get him now?"

Chapter 36

AZHAR AND MOHMED caught up to Warren just as he was going through the front door of the hotel. Azhar smiled. He knew where Steelgrave was staying, and which way he would walk to and from the gallery opening. Looking around, there was an alley across the street and down a-ways. A perfect place to watch the hotel from and better yet, Steelgrave would walk past it going to the gallery.

***

Going into the small hotel, I walked through the lobby and up the stairs to my room on the second floor. I sat at the small desk and took out my phone to call Gino.

"Pronto."

"Gino, it's Warren. Thanks for the text can, you tell me what those two guys asking about me looked like?"

"One was young, maybe twenty-four; he stayed in the car. The one doing the asking; maybe thirty-five. They both had dark hair and could be Middle Eastern."

"Could be?"

"Warren, this is Europe. Many Turks, Southern Italians, and others can look Middle Eastern."

"How were they dressed, and what were they driving?"

"Jeans, with very casual shirts and jogging shoes. They were driving a small white Fiat van. They left, I would guess for Lucca."

"Thanks, Gino."

After hanging up, I thought, "Definitely not FBI, they would never be seen in jeans and jogging shoes driving a van." I looked over to the minibar . . . then at my watch. I had time for a nap; it could be a long night. I started playing the album "Take the Coltrane" on my phone, laidback on the bed, and slipped into a deep meditation. I came out of the meditation feeling great. I looked at my watch; it was just past the hour of the starting of the gallery's opening event. Perfect by the time I showered and got there, it would be half over. I didn't want to be the first one there.

"It's getting late, Azhar, maybe he left out the back?"

Azhar looked at Mohamed with an expression that showed he was in deep thought thinking the same thing.

"We will wait five more minutes. If Steelgrave doesn't come out, we will go over to the gallery. He is just coming out of the hotel."

I walked out of the hotel and stood on the sidewalk. I looked up and down the street. I didn't see anything suspicious, but to my right across the street, the way I had came from the gallery, I did see an alley. I thought for a minute and decided to go left. It was a little longer, but what the hell I had the time.

***

"Take a look, Mohamed, is he coming?"

Mohamed got down on his knees, where it would be harder for Steelgrave to notice him peeking slightly around the corner.

"He is not coming, Azhar. He went the other way and is just going around the corner."

"Quickly, Mohamed, we know where he is going. We can go back the way we came and get there before him. With a little luck, we will have a shorter way and can abduct him a block before he gets there."

They were off at a slow trot.

"Where are you going, Mohamed?"

"This is the street we walked up."

"No, it's not, it's the next street."

After getting turned around and getting lost when they finally got back to the gallery, Warren Steelgrave had already arrived.

***

The gallery looked great. With the other shops closed with their lights off, the gallery all lit up stood out like a full moon rising at dusk. Warren walked in and looked around. The gallery space was about thirty feet by twenty feet, with old hardwood floors that creaked as you walked on them. The overall room lighting was subdued with overhead track lighting that lit the different pieces of art. There were ceramic relief sculptures and paintings on the walls. Smaller ceramics and sculptures were freestanding on pedestals on the floor. The overall look and feel were beautiful and inviting.

There was a good crowd, everyone with a glass of wine and talking in low voices, causing a kind of low murmur. Catherina came across the room with two glasses of wine and handed one to me. With a smile, she said, "What do you think?"

I raised my glass to hers.

"It looks great, Catherina. What great pieces of art."

"All but a few pieces that I have collected over the years are on consignment. Come, let me introduce you to the artists."

Just then, a man stepped up with an outstretched hand.

"Warren Steelgrave, how have you been. Writing, I hope."

"I have been good, and you? You drinking Absinthe tonight, Jack, like at the party last spring?"

Jack laughed and shook his head slightly said, "Not when I have to drive."

"Good to see you, Jack."

"After Catherina shows you around, I want to talk to you about your last book. At the party, you mentioned you were meeting with your editor to go over the final changes. I bought it when it came out, and I thought the ideas expressed in the form of a fiction mystery fascinating. Find me before you leave."

With that, he wandered off, and Catherina and I began mingling with the crowd. Many of the artists had been at the party Maria had taken me to. I was surprised I remembered most of them.

After a few hours, the crowd began to thin out, and I told Catherina I was going to leave. She hugged me with a hug that lingered and had a deeper meaning than most goodnight hugs. She thanked me for coming and asked if she would see me the next day. There was a long pause, then I asked her if she was free for lunch. She was. I said I would come by the gallery at noon. Then I left.

I started walking to my hotel. I got about two blocks when I noticed I was being followed. I stepped into a small coffee bar. I walked through the bar and out the back, turned down the first alley I came to, and ran all the way to the hotel.

I packed and sent a text to Catherina, letting her know I would have to break our lunch date. Something came up, and I had to leave. I would give her a call in a few days and explain.

The next morning, I checked out and went out the back to make my way to my car. I walked out on to the street, looking for them as I left. Surely, one was watching the front and one the back. The trick was to get to my car in a way that took him farther away from their car; if I beat him to my car, by the time they regrouped and went back to their car, I would be long gone. Then what. I couldn't go back to Muriaglio.

Just then, I saw him duck back into a small alley. Calling his buddy, I am sure to give him my location and the direction I was headed. I started running with my backpack, and the chase was on. Lucky for me, I had a long block head start, and my car was only a half-block away.

I got to the car and got in. I started it just as he got there. I pulled away, knocking him down, and I was gone.

Chapter 37

"WHAT NOW, AZHAR?"

"I don't know. Steelgrave won't go back to the village. Let's get a room. I have to think about this. The mission was to find out if Mauro Moretti is alive and helping our enemies. The plan was a quick grabbing up of this Warren Steelgrave to see if he knows. It doesn't make sense to spend a lot of time now to catch him and find out he doesn't have any information. There must be another way to find out what we need." After thinking he went on. "Let's drive to Cremona. I remember that's where the home of Signor Moretti lives, we staked it out once when we wanted to abduct Mauro Moretti the first time. After we can go back to the village and wait for Warren Steelgrave."

"Why there, Azhar?"

"It has only been six months, Mohamed. If Mauro is alive, he would still be recuperating. I bet the family, especially his mom, would keep him close. He only needs the use of a computer to work with the FBI."

Mohamed nodded, he understood, and they headed to the car. It was only two and a half hours from Lucca to Cremona. Once there, it only took Azhar about ten minutes to find the house.

***

I headed out of the city to Florence. While driving, I kept thinking of who would be following me. Then I remembered Jim's call and him asking I contact Signor Moretti. My cousin Gino said possibly, Middle Eastern. They either think I still have the file, or they want what information I do have. Shit, I thought this was over. I pulled over and stopped to make a call to Signor Moretti.

"Pronto."

I recognized the voice. "Gino, this is Warren Steelgrave, Tell Signor Moretti I have Middle Eastern men tailing me. I have given them the slip. He will know what it means." Then I hung up, got back on the road to Florence. Arriving in Florence, I got a room at the Borghese Palace Art Hotel and called Jim Dempsey.

"Hello"

"Jim, it's Warren. Do you have any idea why I have two Middle Eastern men trying to abduct me?"

There was a long pause, then Jim answered, "Nothing that I can think of; let me do some checking, and I will get back to you. This number OK to call?"

"Yeah, it's OK. I will hideout until I hear from you."

I lay back on the bed; then decided to go to dinner.

***

"That's the house, Mohamed, pull over there where the shoulder of the road gets a little wider. We will get a room later. With some luck, we might not be too long."

Mohamed pulled over while Azhar was reaching behind his seat for a pair of binoculars.

"This is good, Mohamed, we can watch the house from here."

"There is a car down the road, Signor Moretti, with two men watching the house."

"Government, Gino?"

"No. One got out for a moment: Middle Eastern."

Signor Moretti sighed and turned to go into his study and said, "Take care of it, Gino."

Gino took his phone out of his coat pocket and made a call.

"Azhar, this is making me nervous. I was told the reason we don't do any operations in Italy is that the Mafia won't allow it. You can't rent a car or apartment, nothing without them knowing, and they put an end to it. I once asked a friend, why? He said because terrorist activity causes too much government attention, and that would be bad for business."

"That's stupid to think that way; it makes no sense."

"We sent a whole team to abduct one man and what happened to the team; they are all dead or in custody. Now we are sitting here watching Signor Moretti's house. I tell you this is not a good idea."

At just that moment, two cars pulled up one in front, one in the rear of the van, blocking them in. Two men got out and walked up to the drivers-side of the van. One tapped on the window and made a gesture with his hand to roll down the window. Mohamed rolled down the window, and both he and Azhar where shot in the head. The doors were opened, and both bodies put in the back of the van. One man got in the driver's seat and drove away.

***

The next morning, I woke up, showered, packed, and decided to walk over to the Café Duomo. I checked out of the hotel and asked them to store my backpack until I returned. It was such a beautiful morning. The sun was

bright, and the air crisp. It took me back to when I was going to school here and first met Cindy. I turned the corner onto via dell'Oriuolo, and there it was the Cattedrale di Santa Maria del Fiori. The morning sun was lighting up the dome as if lit by a spotlight. It is a spectacular sight and one I never get tired of seeing. I continued to Café Duomo and walked in to be greeted with a big smile by Mauro.

"Buongiorno, Warren, it is great to see you!"

"Buongiorno, Mauro, I would like a cappuccino and a brioche, please."

I then walked to the back and sat at the table where I had so many coffees with Cindy. Just as Mauro sat down my coffee, my phone began to buzz. It was from Jim Dempsey.

"Hello, Jim"

"Warren, I just got this information. First, no one has any idea why you might be followed. But this might be related. We are getting some real-time decoded internet chatter. A top lieutenant and another top aid have gone missing in Italy. Mauro's name has come up in some of the chatter. It seems they were trying to get information on Mauro Moretti. These two guys have gone missing and have them really upset. Hope that helps."

"Thanks, Jim, that helps more than you know."

I hung up my phone, took a sip of my coffee, and thought, "I guess my call to Signor Moretti was timely."

Chapter 38

MIKSA WAS SITTING in the kitchen of a small rented house in Tustin, California. It was a small three-bedroom house about three miles from the John Wayne Airport. A team of eight had been renting houses and apartments in the area over the last three months. They all have been taking jobs and blending into the community while making preparations for the Grammy Awards. Miksa was sitting at a small table in the kitchen. He sat back and took a sip of wine. He was very worried; he hadn't heard from Azhar for two days. Both Azhar's and Mohamed's phones went straight to voicemail. What has gone wrong?

There was a knock on the front door. Miksa got up and went to answer it. He opened the door and was taken aback; it was Anjum. Anjum was third to the supreme leader, and Miksa had only met him once. Nervously he said, "Anjum, please come in." Anjum entered the house, and Miksa continued. "Something to drink? I have just opened a very fine wine?"

"Thank you, no. Have you heard from Azhar?"

"No."

"Why was he in Italy? He was supposed to be here."

Miksa went into a long explanation about the rumors of Mauro Moretti being alive and helping the FBI. That he sent Azhar and Mohamed to find out for sure. It should not have taken more than three days.

Anjum sat with his head looking down, patiently waiting for Miksa to finish. When Miksa had finished, he looked up and said, "Miksa, what difference would it make if he is alive or dead? Working with the FBI or not. The information would not change what we have to do. It was extremely dangerous to send the two of them. Now we have to worry if the FBI has them and what information about our plans they are giving up. We sanctioned the attempt to get the protocol. The information would have made a huge difference in the war against the west. But you failed and now this. We have sent a man to call them back as soon as we got the word, they went to Italy instead of here. He is still in Italy trying to find them or what happened to them. I pray for you; they are not in FBI custody."

Just then, Anjum's phone started buzzing. He answered it.

"Yes . . . Are you sure? . . . Be careful but see what you can confirm . . . I understand. I think that is a good idea, then return."

"That was our man in Italy. Mohamed's van was found in an alley. It had a lot of blood and brain matter inside. The rumor on the street is it was a mob killing over something. He is going to pose as a reporter to see what information he can get out of the police." He paused, staring at Miksa, thinking, then he continued. "Many think it was more important to revenge your brother's death than to get information on Mauro Moretti. Who would you kill? The head of the FBI? Any FBI agent? The head of the crime family or some of its members? This is crazy thinking. We took a shot and played our cards and lost the hand. To start a war with a crime family or personalize all this with the FBI only makes our mission harder." Then with a focused voice full of intent and intimidation. He said, "We will never have a similar conversation again; understood?"

Miksa nodded, he understood. Then Anjum said, "You are lucky, Miksa, that it was the mafia that caught these two. They are swift and wouldn't care about getting information for the FBI. They just will not tolerate anyone poking around in their world and would never trust the FBI."

Anjum having finished what he came for left. As his driver drove him away, Miksa was standing in the front doorway watching them leave. Miksa knew he was on very thin ice. As the head of this new cell, revenge would have to wait until after the Grammys. He shut the door and went back to his wine.

Suddenly, there was another knock on the door, and Miksa got up and answered it.

Standing on the porch was a very conservative-looking white man.

"Hello, my name is Bob White. My wife, Sandra, and I live across the street. I was waiting for your company to leave before coming over. I wanted to welcome you to the neighborhood."

With that said, he handed Miksa a Tuna casserole. Miksa took the dish and said,

"Thank you very much, I have just opened a wine. Would you join me in a glass?"

Bob hesitated a moment, then smiled and said, "Sure, thank you."

Bob walked in and followed Miksa to the kitchen and sat at the table.

"Tell your wife I said thank you for the casserole. I am not much of a cook and appreciate it. I have been transferred by my company, Persian Rug Imports, and will not be joined with my wife and two sons until the end of the school year."

After a few minutes of small talk, Bob finished his wine and got up from the table.

"Thank you for the wine . . . ah . . . Miksa? Did I pronounce it right?"

Miksa smiled. "Close enough, Bob."

"We have a barbeque on Saturday. I would love for you to come."

"Thank you, I will."

With that, Bob walked across the street where his wife was peeking out the front window curtains. She was of a suspicious nature and had sent Bob over to gather information on the new neighbor. Bob walked into the house, and she was waiting.

"Well?"

Shaking his head, Bob answered, "Sandra, he seems to be a nice guy. He wanted me to thank you for the casserole."

"That's it. You were gone for fifteen minutes? Why is he alone?"

Bob took in a breath and let out a sigh and smugly answered, "His company transferred him here. His wife and two sons will join him at the end of their school year."

Sandra looked at her husband and with a look of disappointment coupled with a little anger. The look a mother gives her teenage son caught using a finger to scoop a bit of soft butter and eating it.

"What company does he work for?" It's an import company. I forgot the name. "What's his wife's name?" No answer. "What country do they live it?" No answer. "What month is the family coming?' No answer. You didn't find out a thing, did you? He played you, fool."

"Sandra, he did not." Then he said the wrong thing. "Men aren't as snoopy as women. I tell you he is a nice guy. You can drill him Saturday; he said he is coming."

Sandra turned and walked away. Bob stood there and thought, "He was very disarming." Miksa sat back down at the table to finish his wine and thought. "Americans; such fools."

Chapter 39

ABIR GOT TO work just before 9:00 a.m. He parked in lot B and headed into the building to start his workday. The parking lot was wet from rain that morning, and the sky was beginning to clear. It was going to be another beautiful day. What a country. He had never experienced weather like this. The air was so clean and all the contrasting colors; beautiful. He entered the large office on the third floor and walked to his cubical passing Richard Bourn's desk.

"Good morning, Richard."

Richard looked up and nodded. Richard had lost a good friend on 9/11 in the Pentagon building; he didn't trust Abir. He knew in his heart that Abir was still working for the other side. You cannot trust any of them.

Abir sat down at his desk and started going through all the printed-out transcripts in his inbox. He didn't like what he was seeing.

***

Commander Hutson walked into director Nohr's office and sat down in front of his desk.

"Good morning, Commander."

"Good morning, Zac. How is our boy doing?"

"So far, fine. I have been very impressed, and I am beginning to trust Abir. With his help, we have been staying ahead of the terrorists and hardening sites just before they hack them."

"Good. I have to submit a report to the joint chiefs next week; give me your report by tomorrow?"

"It will be on your desk in the morning."

The commander stood and started to leave, saying, "Good. Any time for a round of golf on Saturday?"

Zac looked up; he knew better than to say no. I guess from the years as a spy, Commander Hutson always spoke as if someone was listening to the conversation. What he was saying was there was an important meeting on Saturday, and he was to be there. It was going to take place on the golf course, where it would be almost impossible to bug. This was the real reason for coming in to see him this morning.

"Love to; what time?"

"We have a 9:00 a.m. tee time."

"See you at nine, John."

Hutson nodded and left.

We . . . thought Zac? Who else would be there?

Just at that moment, his computer dinged. He had received a message from Abir. "Sir, can you come down; there is something I need to discuss."

Zac thought for a moment. "This must be important; in the past, he has caught Richard eavesdropping." He emailed back. Please come up to my office.

After a few minutes, Abir walked into the office. Zac looked up as Abir entered and was amazed at how quickly Abir was becoming Americanized. Standing there in tan dockers, brown loafers, and a blue plaid short-sleeve shirt, sporting a new apple watch and a new short haircut. He was surely embracing the American dream.

Zac motioned with a hand gesture to take a seat in one of the chairs in front of the desk. Zac was beginning to like this guy.

"Thank you, sir. When I got in this morning, they brought me a very recent transcript. I noticed this phrase that I have highlighted." Sliding a page across the desk to Zac, he went on. "It is a very unusual phrase to use; I had seen it used before. I did a data search for the phrase through saved transcripts for the last month. I found it in these three." Abir slid the three sheets of paper over to Zac. "Together, they make sense. I have typed up a sheet for you, combining the phrases into the main topic of all the sheets and translated for you in English."

Abir waited as Zac read over the last sheet. Then go back and look over the other sheets and reread the translated sheet. At first, the expression on Zac's face was one of curiosity, then turned to concern.

"They have something big that they want to execute in the coming months. As you can see, sir, they have figured out that we either have the protocol or have Mauro helping us, so they are adjusting. The new plan is to keep going after big targets, power grids, etcetera, to keep our focus away from their main target. My guess is it's a smaller soft target. Something they have already penetrated or know they can very easily." Abir waited while Zac digested the information.

"They are very smart, Abir. We have all our resources divided. Eighty percent are hardening all of our industries in order of importance, starting with national security systems. The rest is going through the systems of private industries, starting with the banking system."

"Sir, if I may, I would like to offer an opinion to consider." Zac nodded for him to go on. "I don't think that they have the capability to do damage to our . . . America's major systems. What needs to be done is to find the intended target."

"That could be anything, Abir."

"Now that we at least know their intentions, we can spare some of the manpower to the effort."

Zac sat there, Abir's slips in the use of the language didn't go unnoticed. Catching himself and changing our, to America's major systems and the use of we.

"Tell me, Abir, how is the family getting along?"

"Well. America is so different from Iraq. Everything from the weather to shopping malls. It was overwhelming at first. The girls adjusted quickly to the shopping. We all keep America in our prayers every day. None of us could conceive of such a place. We have been truly blessed."

"I am glad to hear that."

Abir stood, straightened his chair, and left. Zac was no fool, and yet Abir seemed so genuine. But still, he was working with a group to harm America, and many felt he should be in jail for what he had done. He has been a great asset to our cause. Or is he a double agent?

"Where have you been, Abir?"

"I was asked to go to Mr. Nohr's office, Richard."

"By who?"

"I think you should ask Mr. Nohr if you have more questions, Richard."

Abir sat at his desk, and it felt different in some way. He wondered if Richard had gone through his desk while he was gone. He looked around. There were four other cubicles in the large office; he could ask someone if they had seen anyone at his desk. Then he laughed to himself, of course, someone had gone through his desk and his car in the parking lot every chance they got. He was not trusted. If the positions were swapped, he would do the same. Still, it was different from Richard. Richard did not like him. He would have to be careful not to be set up.

Chapter 40

I WOKE UP AND looked at my phone to see what time it was: 8:00 a.m. I never sleep this late. I also had a text from Maria. "Arrived back home last night, text me back when you get this."

I texted back, "I am in Florence and just woke up; do you want to do something together today?"

"How about you come by for a coffee and a small bite of something, and we can discuss it."

I looked at the time on my phone and texted back, "Great; be there by 9:30."

I checked out of the hotel and drove over to Maria's apartment house. I felt confident I was not being followed; it would take them a while to regroup and figure out where in Italy I am. Maria buzzed me in, and as I started up the stairs, there she was leaning on the banister a floor above me smiling. She was wearing a white sundress with black sandals: She looked terrific as always.

I got to the top of the stairs, and we embraced and kissed. "Come in, Warren, I will prepare two coffees for us on the balcony. Please go on out to the balcony, and I will bring the coffee. I walked out and sat down at the small table. In the center of the table was a large plate with some fruit, cheese, prosciutto, and two cornettos.

The view of Florence was spectacular. The city shined in the clear morning light. There were just a few large cumulus clouds on a dark blue sky sitting just above the Ponte Vecchio. Just then, she walked out with the two espressos and set them on the table.

"Coffee corrector?"

"No, thank you, Maria." I took a small plate and put on it some fruit and a cornetto and asked, "How is your father, Maria?"

She shrugged her shoulders and became a little melancholy "He is OK. It's his heart. It's beginning to fail because of his age. There is nothing that can be done, and we are all a little depressed as we come to grips with it. You think you are prepared for losing a parent, but in the end, you are not."

There is nothing that can be said at times like this. I reached across the table and took her hand; she looked up, and with a slight smile, she let me know she knew I understood.

We sat in silence, each lost in our thoughts having our breakfast. Then I broke the silence. "What would you like to do today?"

"Today, Warren . . . I would like to go to Siena for the day; then come home and make love to you." Then with a smile, she went on. "Not necessarily in that order."

I finished my coffee, stood, and walked around the small table to help her out of her chair. She took my hand and led me to the bedroom. We entered the bedroom, and

I looked around. The bed cover was turned down neatly, and a large vase of flowers on the dresser was giving the room a lite but wonderful smell. The lace window curtains were drawn. The morning light coming through the lace put the room in a low romantic light. This was surely thought out.

I pulled her close and kissed her neck, taking in her scent mixed with the scent of soap and just-washed hair. I could feel her excitement begin to rise as my right hand slid over her ass and started unfastening her dress. Her dress fell to the floor and still kissing her, I unfastened her bra and laid her back on the bed. She lay there in her panties as I undressed. I laid down beside her and started kissing her breasts very slowly, making my way down her body. She reached down and took off her panty and spread her legs as I reached my goal.

Afterward, we lay there in each other's arms, not saying a word, just enjoying the embrace. Finally, I half sat up on one arm and said, "Shall we shower and head to Siena for lunch?"

She smiled and nodded, she agreed. We showered, made the bed, did the morning dishes, and were out the door to my car.

We arrived in Siena a little after midday and parked in Parcheggio il Campo on Via pier Andrea Mattioli. We took our time walking through the city, enjoying the architecture and shops making our way to the Duomo di Siena.

We found a little place to eat just off Via del Capitano, named the Osteria Permalico. "Maria, Cindy is going to provide me with two tickets to this year's Grammys. I have not

mentioned it to you because I wasn't sure I wanted to attend. Would you like to go? You could spend a couple of weeks. I could show you San Francisco and Lake Tahoe. What do you think?"

Maria turned and looked over the city. I could feel her reluctance to the idea and wasn't expecting that. After a few moments, she turned to face me and said, "Warren, the Grammys are something special for you and Cindy. I think I would be in the way."

At that moment, I realized what was being said to me. If Cindy were truly out of my system, I would not be considering going to the Grammys. Going was just a way to maintain the relationship. What did Maria want from me?

I can't rewrite my history. Cindy is at the least a friend. And, yes, I have supported her emotionally in obtaining her life's dream. I would like to be there in hopes of her receiving a Grammy; I won't apologize or feel remotely guilty for the support of someone who has never wronged me.

"Maria, I understand. I hope you think about it. I can always take one of my daughters. After lunch, I would like to walk to the Duomo."

"OK."

We finished lunch and walked the three blocks to the Duomo. We rounded the corner and there it was. I have been here three times before and get overwhelmed every time I enter it.

We spent the rest of the day walking the streets and alleys of Siena. We found a small restaurant for dinner near the Palazzo Pubblico: Ristorante Pizzeria Spadaforte. We ate outside overlooking the Piazza del Campo, one of Europe's greatest medieval squares, where the famous

Palio di Siena is run. We just finished eating when my phone began to buzz. I looked at it was Jim Dempsey.

"Excuse me, Maria, I have to take this."

I got up and walked to the street.

"What's up, Jim?"

"I have a little more information on the two guys who were following you. They were snooping around Signor Moretti's house. Never a good idea. They were freelancing and not supposed to be there. I wanted to let you know you don't have to be concerned anymore."

"Thanks, Jim, I appreciate the call."

"Not a problem."

I ended the call and walked back to the table.

"Everything OK, Warren?"

"Yes, it was Jim following up on our visit to Signor Moretti. He just wanted to say thanks. I guess it turned out positive."

Chapter 41

I SPENT THE REST of the week in Florence with Maria. We didn't do much, I would go to work with her. She had an office not far from Café Duomo on Via Camillo. It was on the third floor of a building facing the street. I would use a small spare office to write. We would go to dinner after work and walk the city. Ever since Siena, there seemed to be a growing distance between us. The fact I was in contact with Cindy and was going to the Grammys bothered her in a way I didn't understand: hell, I'm not sure she even understands. On Monday, I headed home to Muriaglio.

Being home in Muriaglio Maria and I would talk maybe twice a week. One day she called, knowing I was preparing to go back to America until spring.

"Hello."

"Good morning, Warren. When do you leave for America?"

"Monday."

"If the offer still stands, I would like to come and join you and go to the Grammys?'

"That would be fantastic. Will you be coming with me now?"

"No. I thought I would come the two weeks before the Grammys and stay a couple of weeks after. I have a lot to do around here first."

We talked about things going on in each of our personal lives for about fifteen minutes then ended the call. I made myself a coffee and went out on the deck to sit and enjoy it. I was glad Maria was coming to stay in America for an extended time. If this relationship was to go to the next level, it would involve her living in America part of the year. Although not mentioned, that was what this trip was about; a trial run, and we both knew it.

My phone began to buzz. I picked it up, it was my agent, Mike Sucato.

"Hello."

"Warren, it's Mike. I have you booked for some interviews and book signings over the next month."

"Mike, we have talked about this. I agreed to the one next week, but that was it. You know I hate this sort of thing. It takes up too much of my time. It's like having a job."

"I know it's just a few, and they are all local. I will send you the list. See you next week."

I ended the call and finished my coffee, letting my irritation go. I write for the enjoyment of writing. I don't need the money or a fulltime job. I understand Mike is in a different situation and needs to sell books to add to his income stream and interviews and book signings sell books. I looked at my watch; it was time to head to Castellamonte for lunch at the Tre Re. I was meeting a beautiful woman from my bank to go over my accounts before I leave.

I arrived in San Francisco at 2:30 in the afternoon, and my daughter Sherry was there to pick me up at the airport and take me home. I'm always amazed at how much things change when you are gone for six months. We made our way across the San Mateo bridge to Hayward, where I was born and lived most of my life.

"Dad, what were you planning for dinner?"

"Haven't thought about it."

"Your grandchildren have missed you and are waiting at the house. I thought we could order pizza."

"Perfect."

We arrived at my house where Robert and the girls were waiting. Arriving home, I always feel a little melancholy. I have lived in this house for almost forty years, and all the memories flood back: the children growing up here, all the Thanksgiving dinners, and all the family gatherings with friends and family that are no longer alive. Very deep roots.

As I walked up the stairs to the front door, I look for Anne in the window. Anne was my dog for many years; we were inseparable. She passed just before I started living in Italy. She would always be looking out the window for me to return. It's a habit I can't seem to shake. Whenever I start up the stairs, I look for her in the window. Sometimes she is there for just a brief moment.

The rest of the evening, we ate pizza and caught up. The melancholy starts to leave, and it's good to be home for a while.

On Thursday, I drove to KQED, a local TV station in Oakland, California, about fifteen minutes from my house for a TV interview. It was going to be a taped interview, which is always nice. I have the right to view and correct any mistakes. The interview went well, and they were going to air it nationally next week.

I was sitting on the deck in my backyard alone and missing having a dog to share the beautiful afternoon. I had just poured myself my first martini in seven months and was thoroughly enjoying it. I found it easy to give up the alcohol and figured although it was getting out of hand and it was good to stop for a while, it was not a problem. Just as I lit my cigar, my phone buzzed. I picked it up; it was Cindy.

"Hello"

"Hello, Warren, I saw your interview last night on TV. I wanted to call to congratulate you on your new book. I got your email; thanks for confirming you are going to be at the Grammys. It wouldn't be the same without knowing you were in attendance."

We talked for only a few minutes more before we hung up. I looked at the martini and drank it down in one motion and got up and made a second one.

***

Miksa was watching my interview on T.V. when his new lieutenant Abbud came in with some memos for him and set them on the table. Abbud stood watching, wondering what was so interesting to Miksa about this interview. Miksa looked up and said, "Have a seat Abbud. Do you know this person being interviewed?"

"No. Should I?"

"He is a writer. The interviewer asked him if his books were autobiographical. He wasn't clear with the answer.

He said, in his opinion, all good writers leave part of themselves in their writing. That you should be able to read the book and know the writer. Then the interviewer went on to ask him about his association with the FBI and the Mafia. Again, he sidestepped the question. I want you to go buy all his books for me to read."

"Why, Miksa?"

"This is Warren Steelgrave. He was the man Azhar went to Italy to abduct. He also lives north of here part of the year at his home in the Bay Area. He is living there now."

Chapter 42

MIKSA SPENT THE next week reading Warren Steelgrave's books. There were four in a series about a writer who gets pulled into different scenarios involving the FBI and in the second book, a powerful crime family. In one of the books, the main character has a love interest who, through the series, becomes a well-known singer-songwriter.

Miksa decided to do a Google search on Warren Steelgrave and found an article about his daughter's wedding and Warren Steelgrave's life being saved by his girlfriend: Cindy O'Brian. Cindy, a singer-songwriter, had just released her second album. Miksa now saw the connection to the FBI and the Moretti family. He decided to call, Anjum.

"Hello."

"Anjum, it's, Miksa." It was silent. Anjum was waiting for Miksa to go on. "Anjum, everything is moving on schedule. I'm awfully bored, and I am afraid I might be raising suspicions with the neighbors. I thought I would take a few days and travel north to San Francisco. I have never been there and would like to see it. We have talked in the past of targets there, and I would like to familiarize myself with the area."

Anjum didn't like the idea; it was only six weeks to the Grammys and felt Miksa had an agenda he wasn't saying.

"How long will you be gone, Miksa?"

"I will leave tomorrow, Thursday, and return Monday."

"Miksa, we are close to the Grammys. No trouble; not even a speeding ticket."

"I understand." Miksa hung up and started packing a bag.

The next morning, Miksa was putting his bag in the car when Mrs. White walks across the street.

"Good morning, Miksa, going somewhere?"

"Good morning, Mrs. White. I am going to San Jose to visit some relatives."

"I have friends in San Jose, what area?"

This caught Miksa by surprise. He had no knowledge of San Jose. He just remembered seeing it in the news and that it was somewhere in the Bay Area.

"I should kill this snoopy bitch," Miksa thought.

"Near the airport. I am sorry, Mrs. White, but I need to get going; I'm awful late in leaving." With that, he got into the car and left. "What is it with American women don't they know their place. This is a disgusting culture."

Miksa made his way through town and got onto the 101 Freeway North. He headed north until he got to Interstate Five, then settled back for the six-hour drive to Hayward, California, and the home of Warren Steelgrave.

***

Abir got up from his desk, got his keys, and was headed home for the evening. He said goodnight to Richard as he left, he wondered who was following him tonight. He got to his car, and on the drive home, he started thinking about all the pressure on the family being constantly monitored every minute of every day. The children weren't aware because it was never discussed, but it was beginning to get to his wife. He had to keep reminding her if the tables were turned and he was caught by Isis working for the Americans, he would be dead, and she and the girls would be used for sexual pleasures of the soldiers. He was lucky he wasn't at Guantanamo, and the wife and girls still in Iraq. All in all, he gave thanks to God every day and asked to be shown a way to show his appreciation to the Americans and earn their trust. If he didn't, he wondered what would happen to him once his usefulness ran out.

Arriving home and entering the house, his two girls ran and gave him hugs. His wife stepped out of the kitchen and said, "Dinner is ready. Wash up and come and eat."

Abir could tell she was upset, but it would have to wait until later when the girls were upstairs finishing their homework.

After the dishes were done and Abir had helped with the math homework, and the girls were bathed, and in bed, it was the time set aside every night he and his wife would spend together.

Abir started the conversation, "Why are you upset, my dear?"

"The girls were teased and harassed again today."

"They didn't mention it to me."

"They won't, Abir. They don't want you to worry. It's always the same three girls. I should go to the parents or the school, but I too am afraid it might be seen as ungrateful and complaining by your bosses and cause the family more harm."

Abir nodded, he understood and thought about the hatred he felt from Richard, then said, "I will talk to my main boss. We seem to have fostered a kind of respect for each other. I will ask for his advice."

The next day, Abir went to the top floor, got off the elevator, and walked down the hall to Zac Nohr's office. He found the door open and knocked on the doorframe.

"Come in."

Abir walked through the door and stood there. Zac Nohr looked up from his work and stared for a moment, trying to remember the correct pronunciation of Abir's name.

"Have a seat, Abir."

Abir walked in and sat in one of the chairs in front of the large wooden desk.

"What's on your mind?"

Abir proceeded to explain the situation at school with his two girls.

"Sir, my wife, and I are extremely grateful for being here in America. We understand why people treat us as they do, but our children do not. Because we are grateful and don't want to cause you any difficulties, I need your advice on how to best handle this situation. Zac leaned back in his chair with his hands laced together behind his head to think. He knew that to get involved with the personal matters of someone who not too long ago was on the other side and considered a terrorist would be suicide for his career. The blowback would be terrible for him and his family. Yet, Abir has been a great asset so far, and if this goes unchecked, this could escalate into something as bad if it were found out that he was once a terrorist placed by the FBI in a neighborhood and his children allowed to go to the neighborhood school.

"Abir, sometimes children work these things out on their own. Give it a few weeks and report back to me."

Abir nodded, he understood, got up, and left. Zac had a plan; it was lucky that the principal of that school was his sister. He picked up the phone and placed a call.

"Sis, it's me. What? . . . I have been busy, and I thought Linda had called; we will be there Saturday for Joey's birthday. The reason I'm calling I have a problem I need you to handle. It has to be done without involving the parents of two Iraqi students being bullied. I know you can find a way to stop this quietly, very quietly. . . I will get you the names . . . of course it's a matter of national security. . . Don't ask anymore questions. I can't give you detail. Thanks, Sis, you're the greatest."

Chapter 43

ABIR WALKED INTO his office area, and as he walked to his desk, he could feel the watchful stare of Richard following him to his desk. This seemed to him a little more than the watchful eyes and surveillance he was encountering from all the others. This seemed to be more personal as if his presence was causing Richard a personal problem.

Abir sat down at his desk, and then it came to him: an extreme idea. "What if Richard was selling information and Abir's presence, causing extra surveillance was putting Richard's activities at risk. Richard would have to set him up and get rid of him. It was a farfetched idea; still, he would have to take extra precautions. If the last five years have taught him anything, it was life can be stranger than fiction."

***

Miksa drove straight to Hayward, stopping only for gas. With the internet, it is very easy to find someone's address

these days, and Miksa drove straight to the street Warren
Steelgrave lived on. He was impressed with the size of the
house. It was a short way from the street on a small hill.
It was near the end on a dead-end street, making it very
hard for someone to escape.

He parked his car at the end of the street and waited.
Soon the garage-door raised up, and Warren Steelgrave
came out with a small overnight bag, put it in the trunk, and
drove off. "He must be going somewhere for the weekend,"
thought Miksa. It doesn't matter; he would scout the area
and come up with a plan for dealing with Steelgrave after
the Grammys.

Hayward was small compared to Los Angeles; it would
be easy to set a trap and kill Warren Steelgrave. After having
something to eat downtown, he headed back to Tustin.

Miksa was driving back to Tustin when his phone
buzzed.

"Hello?"

"Miksa it's Anjum, when will you back?"

"I'm on my way now and will be back in about two hours."

"Go straight to the meeting place; we will be waiting. We have found Abir."

Miksa knew Abir was the one that was the traitor and was working with the FBI. The whole way back to Tustin, he thought of Abir and his betrayal of the cause. Finally, he pulled into the parking lot of the Persian Rug Imports office building. It was a small nondescript two-story building in a small industrial section of town near the airport. Anjum ran the import business out of the space, and it was used to launder money for Allah's Army. It was an internet type of business. No employees, no trucks, or inventory.

Miksa was the last to arrive. They all gathered around a large conference table on the second floor, and when Miksa sat down, Anjum began, "I have called this meeting to discuss a message I received today. It comes from our base in Iran. Our Russian allies have sent up through channels information they have received from an American mole. The Americans have Abir in custody, and he is helping in their efforts to harden targets that we are trying to gain access to. We are getting too close to the Grammys to make a slip. All information and messages about that operation will be communicated through handwritten messages delivered by one of our messengers. All coded emails will be about other attacks. It's time to give them some information that will give them something to focus on that will keep them away from finding our true target. How soon before the bomb is ready?"

Miksa answered, "About three weeks, we have all the components and only have to assemble it."

"Good. I would like it ready and available to put in place at the first opportunity. We can target a power outage the day before the Grammys. We have someone working in receiving. As all the staging and other equipment are being received, we will create the outage for about four hours. This will put them behind schedule, and the deliveries backed up in the receiving areas. It's our man in the field who has the responsibility to see how the mid-sized crates are being checked through security and find a way to get ours through and placed under the stage. Any questions?"

There were no questions, and the meeting ended with everyone leaving.

"Miksa, would you wait a minute. I want to talk to you."

Miksa was nervous whenever Anjum wanted to talk to him alone.

"Miksa, I have an assignment for you. Abir was part of your brother's cell. Did you have a lot of dealings with him?"

"Yes."

"I want you to head up finding a target on the East Coast and sending out information in your old code as a diversion. I'm sure Abir will recognize it and decode it for the FBI. I will send you the addresses of those that will help you as soon as I'm sure I can trust them."

Miksa nodded; he understood and left to go home.

Anjum also saw the Warren Steelgrave interview and knew he was home just up the coast. He knew where Miksa was during the last couple of days. It worried him that Steelgrave would turn up this close to the Grammys and to hear that Abir was working with the FBI. He was certain it was no coincidence; Steelgrave must still be working with the FBI. Maybe Miksa was correct in thinking Steelgrave should be picked up.

He couldn't mention this to Miksa; he was too emotionally connected to the situation. He would send a two-man team to keep an eye on Steelgrave and to monitor his phones. He would gather more information before deciding what to do. If they were to pick up Steelgrave now, it would put a focus on this area of the country and could expose what they have been doing. The thing to do was to keep an eye on Steelgrave and make sure what, if anything, he is up to. If he is working for the FBI, they could kill him closer to the Grammys.

Chapter 44

ABIR STARTED SEARCHING the dark web every chance he had. He would stay late, finishing his work for the FBI so he could search during the day at work. He knew he was being watched, so he would make it look as if it were part of the work for the FBI. He knew what would happen if he was caught doing it on a private computer.

He got an email from Zac Nohr requesting he come up to his office. When Abir walked in, he was greeted by Director Nohr and another man he did not know and wasn't introduced to.

"Abir, what the hell have you been doing on the dark web?"

"Sir, I have been searching for a mole."

"On who's orders?"

"On my own, sir. I have noticed in the transcripts that I have been given some things that lead me to believe I have been found out. Nothing concrete, but I wanted to search on my own. I have found evidence today the Russians have penetrated our system. I have no proof yet, but I believe they have passed on to Iran information about me. I was going to come to you as soon as I was sure."

"Abir, come over here and sit at this computer and show this man what you have."

Abir sat down and went to the dark web. Using certain code words and protocols, he was deep in the web and on a very secure site that exchanged messages. The messages themselves were in another weird code. Even when Abir would translate and decode, they had a kind of double meaning, and unless it was a message you were waiting for, you wouldn't know the meaning. Finally, he found a conversation between two terrorists he could interpret.

"Here, I know these two, and they have always been lazy and sloppy. One wants to know if the information the mole had given the Russians on the Iraqi is accurate."

The person that was never introduced looked at Director Nohr with a look that spoke volumes.

"Abir, have you spoke to any others about this?"

"No, sir."

"Don't. Just go back to your regular duties."

With that, Abir got up and left to go back to his cubical. After he was gone, Director Nohr turned to the other man in the room and asked, "What do you think?"

"I think you have a mole in this division. The questions are, for how long and what kind of information has he or she been selling to the Russians? The good news is that the people that know Abir is here and working for us have just been found out. We will know shortly who; it will take longer to build a case against them. Let me get started on it. I will keep you in the loop."

He reached out and shook Director Nohr's hand and left.

Zac sat down at his desk. How lucky they were to have Abir, but what was going to happen to him in the long run? Would he ever be able to live a normal life in America? Here is a guy very grateful for America, and among others in his division is an American with top clearances betraying his country for money.

He looked at his watch. It was early; still, he was going home and spend time with his family and get drunk.

Abir sat at his desk and went back to work when Richard walked up to his desk.

"Where did you go, Abir?"

"I don't report to you, Richard. I told you before if you have a problem with me or my work take it up with the director."

"There is something odd with this guy, always watching and going through my stuff to see what I am up to," thought Abir. Abir worked the rest of the day on translating transcripts he had received.

When he got home, there seemed to be a better mood in the house, not so much tension. After the girls had gone to bed, he and his wife sat together with a cup of tea for their daily time together.

"How was your work today, Abir?"

"It was a typical day. Did something happen the girls seemed different tonight?"

"In what way?"

"I can't say . . . more relaxed less tension, I guess."

"There has been no bullying this week I was going to say something yesterday but thought I better wait and give it a little more time."

Abir looked over at his wife with a content look on his face and a smile and thought, "Zac Nohr, this was someone he could trust." He liked Zac a lot.

***

I was returning home after visiting my daughter Stephanie and friends in the San Luis Obispo area on the central coast of California. I had just gotten home and was taking my bag out of the car when my neighbor walking her dog stopped to say hi. "Good morning, Mary."

"Good morning, Warren. How long are you going to be here before you head back to Italy?"

"I will be home until sometime late spring."

"It's nice to have you back. You were gone all last week, Mr. Harris has your mail."

Mary knew all that happens in the neighborhood and was trying to find out where I had been.

"I went down to see my daughter for a week. She and the family are all good."

"You missed the excitement last week." Kind of laughing, she went on. "There was this man parked on the street for a couple of hours. You know how Mrs. Murphy is. After a while, she called the police. It took them forever to send a car. When they got here, the man was gone. She had a fit. For several days, the mystery man was all she would talk about. Finally, I said to her, Linda Murphy, you need a hobby."

"Well, Mary, it's not all bad to have her keeping an eye on the street."

"But, Warren, to hear her tell the story, the man was a terrorist waiting to nab someone."

I picked up my bag and said I had to go in and make a call to my editor, and headed up the steps to the house. Once inside, I set my bag down and went straight to the recorded, saved video. I started checking the video from the front yard camera. I started with the day I left and continued day by day until I came to one that showed part of a car. It was on the day I left.

The car was parked on the opposite side of the street, facing my house. All that was in the video was part of the front license plate. It left about an hour after I did.

I wrote down the number and called Jim Dempsey.

"Hello?"

"Jim, it's Warren. I need a favor. I need a license plate number traced."

"Why, Warren? Care to tell me what's this all about?"

"Probably nothing, Jim. After having those last two following me, I'm maybe a little too cautious."

"Give me the number and any description of the car. I'll get back to you later today."

Chapter 45

LATER THAT SAME day, I received an email. "The license number is for a car registered to a company in Southern California: Persian Rug Imports."

I thought for a moment and decided it was just an outside salesman lost with a wrong address and had pulled over to call and get a correct address and directions. It happened to me many times. I called my daughter Sherry and asked if she was still on for a late lunch. She was, and we agreed to meet at a small restaurant, Nonni's Bistro, in Pleasanton.

I left the house, got into the car, and drove down the street. I made a left at the corner and then another left onto the main street headed for the freeway. As I made the last left from the only outlet from the neighborhood, a green Ford parked on the main street caught my attention. I thought I saw movement in the car, someone bending down so as not to be seen, to make the car seem empty. It was one of those little things that would get bookmarked in my memory as something important.

I got to the restaurant early and had a bourbon old fashioned while I waited for Sherry. When I return from

Italy, I always make it a point to see all the children and catch up with them on what was going on in their lives.

Leaving the restaurant, we said our goodbyes, and as I was about to jaywalk to my car across the street, I looked both ways for traffic. Down the street on the same side as my car, there it was: a green Ford. I got to my car, got in, and started it. The car was parked almost a full block behind me on the same side of the street. How to make sure it was the same car I had seen when leaving home. I pulled out into traffic and kept watching in my mirror to see if the car pulled out; it didn't appear to. I got home and sat out on the back deck. I would keep a close eye on things. Maybe I was still a little jumpy after what happened in Lucca.

***

Anjum's phone buzzed: "Hello?"

"Anjum, it's, Fadil. We have been following Steelgrave for the last week. I see no sign that he is working with the FBI. We have tapped all his calls and other than his children and one friend: nothing. What do you want us to do?"

"You sure he hasn't seen you and is aware that he is being monitored, and you have captured all his calls?"

"The first day we were concerned he might have seen us, but no, he hasn't seen the tail. We are sure we have captured every call. It took us a while on the first day to park close enough to hack into his Wi-Fi and plant the trap on his phone. There has been nothing. I tell you he is not working with anyone."

"Good. Come back. If Steelgrave should see you following, he might call the FBI, causing them to start looking into why. We don't need the attention this close to the Grammys."

***

It's been two weeks, and still, something about that green car is bugging me. I went upstairs to my desk and found the piece of paper with the car license plate number and company name I wrote on. My oldest son John and his family live near Los Angeles, maybe I should visit them. I picked up the phone and gave him a call.

"Hello."

"John, it's Dad. How is the family?"

"Good Dad, are you in Italy or in Hayward?"

"Hayward. I thought I would come down and spend the weekend and catch up if you are going to be home?"

"We have nothing planned, and the boys would love to see you. I will have Sally prepare the spare bedroom. When will you be here?"

"I will fly and rent a car. I have a little business to take care of just south of you. I will plan to be at your house by 7:00 on Friday evening. I will text you if that should change."

"Great, Dad, see you Friday."

I ended the call and put the phone down and started the computer. It was time to checkout "Persian Rug Imports." I was finding it hard to get much information on them. You couldn't order any product from them online or a catalog. It appeared they sold wholesale only. The website itself was simple and gave little information. Not all that unusual but still troubling. I sat back in my chair to think. Who do I know that could contact them as a potential buyer without raising suspicions? Of course: Jim Marino.

I picked up the phone and gave him a call. He answered on the first ring.

"Well, where the hell are you these days, Warren?"

"I am at home. How is the family?"

"All is good here, and yours?"

"All fine. I have been visiting all the kids since I have been back. I am going down to Los Angeles to visit John this weekend. How about we get together for dinner when I get back?"

"That would be great."

"I think it will be easier for me to meet your schedule. Send me some dates that work for you."

"I will."

"One more thing, Jim. I need you to check out a rug company. I will send you an email with all the information on them I have. They are in Tustin, California. I was going by there while I am in the area this weekend."

"Will do, and I will include some dates for dinner."

We ended the call, and I put the phone down. I turned to the computer and made my arrangements for the weekend. I would fly into John Wayne airport early Friday morning. Then drive by Persian Rug Imports to satisfy my curiosity; then up to John's house for the weekend.

Chapter 46

MY PLANE LANDED on time at 9:00 a.m. I had my
rental car and was on my way by 9:30. Tustin
was not far from the airport, and I was driving
by Persian Rug Imports within fifteen minutes. It was
located in a small industrial section of town. It was the
typical industrial park; all the buildings were concrete tilt-
ups about five thousand square feet, all located in an area
about six blocks square. I drove by, and it appeared deserted.
I drove around the block and parked near a corner of a
side street under a tree. From this vantage point, I could
observe the front door and parking lot. The parking lot was
empty of cars, and it looked like no one was there.

My phone went off, an email from Jim Marino, finally.
I opened the email and began to read. Persian Rug Imports
was a private corporation; therefore, no sales volume to
report. They are registered with the state of California
as of last year, with no directors, and the president listed
was an Anjum Sadiq. Other than the information on their
website, Jim had nothing more to add. I sat there thinking,
"This company has only been in existence for about ten
months and appears to have no employees unless they work

nights because of the time difference with the Middle East. Something is not right." After sitting there for about fifteen minutes, I decided to get out of my car and walk over to a small deli across the street.

I walked into the deli and up to the counter, and an elderly black man was doing some cleaning. He was tall, maybe 5'11". He walked up to counter, drying his hands with a towel, and studying me. His voice was deep and deliberate as he asked, "Can I help you?"

"I would like a toasted bagel with lox and cream cheese and a large coffee."

"For here or to go?"

"For here."

"Have a seat. I will bring it to you."

I walked over and took a seat at a table with a window; it had a clear view of Persian Rug Imports. He brought over my order, and I could tell he had been watching me look out the window; he was nobody's fool. He set down my order, and as he started to leave, I asked, "Do you get much business from Persian Rug Imports?"

He smiled and thought a while; he was looking me over, then said, "They owe you money?"

It was his way of letting me know he knew I was watching the building. He must have seen me pull up across the street and sit in the car watching before coming in. I responded by raising one eyebrow with a slight tilt of the head communicating, maybe, but I can't say. He thought for a moment, carefully arranging his words. He knew what he wanted to say without saying it. Finally, his eyes narrowed, and with a slow and deliberate voice, he responded, "Not too often. Always late afternoon, never anything with pork."

I could tell he had been suspicious of that building a long time and was glad it had raised suspicions of others. I smiled; I understood and turned my attention to my bagel and coffee with an eye on Persian Rug Imports.

I was just finishing my coffee when two cars pulled into the parking lot of Persian Rug Imports. One was the car on my home video. I finished my coffee and got up to pay my bill. He handed me back a five-dollar bill in change; as I started to take it, he hung on to it a second. I looked up, and he smiled, gave me a nod, and let go. His way of letting me know he approved. I left the deli and walked over to my car to assume my post.

While I was waiting, I called Jim Marino. He answered on the first ring.

"Warren, I guess you got my email?"

"I did."

"Sorry, it wasn't much help."

"It was. Let me ask if there is any way to check if this company has any employees. Is there any way to access work visa, or rental agreements and such to find out?"

"Warren, what is this all about?"

"There was a car parked on my street several weeks ago. I had the plate ran, and it led me to this place. I'm probably still a little paranoid from what happened in Lucca. I have Maria coming next week for a month, and I want to put this uneasy feeling to rest before she gets here."

"Sounds to me like you are a little bored and looking for something to do. Let me do some checking. It might take a while."

"Thanks, Jim. I will email back a date for dinner next week. I want to confirm which day Maria arrives."

I looked up, and the car in my home video was leaving. I ended the call and decided to follow it. After a few miles through residential neighborhoods, he stopped in front of a house and waited. Within a minute, two men who looked Middle Eastern came out and got into the car, and they drove off. I wrote down the address and continued to follow. After a few miles, they arrived at a house and drove into the driveway. I was a ways back and pulled over to the curb and parked. After a few moments, a middle-aged woman came out of the house from across the street and started watering the flowerbed in front of her house. It was obvious she was watching through the window when they arrived. She was using the watering as an excuse to keep an eye on the house. Every neighborhood had one; the self-appointed neighborhood watch commander. I bet she keeps a written log of all that goes on with that house. I sat and watched for about a half-hour. I was trying to figure a way I could talk to her. Finally, I gave up the idea and wrote down both addresses and left. I headed north to my son's house. My son lived in Thousand Oaks, about an hour and a half away. I stopped for a coffee when my phone buzzed; it was Maria.

"Ciao, Maria. What's up?"

I have made my plane reservations. I will email them to you. I will arrive on Tuesday of next week."

"Great. If you don't mind, I thought we would have dinner with Jim Marino and his wife Kate; you met them at the baptism."

"Yes, I remember I liked them a lot; it will be good to see them again. I have to go; see you on Tuesday. Ciao."

"Ciao."

I finished my coffee and headed on to my son's house.

Chapter 47

I ARRIVED AT MY son's house in the late afternoon. He had just gotten home from work, and his wife was picking up their twin boys from school. We talked late into the night. Just as I was going to bed, I received an email from Jim Marino. All it said was I have the information, but we need to talk. I said goodnight and walked into the guest room. I sat on the edge of the bed and called Jim.

"Warren, I'm glad you called. You want to tell me what kind of trouble you are getting into?"

"None, that I know of. I told you that the car outside my house spooked me. It's probably nothing, Jim."

"I had to pull a few favors at the State Department and have my team do some hacking into a government database, but I got you some answers. In the last three months, eight individuals received visas and temporary work visas for working in the United States. They were issued over the three months. Two from Pakistan, four from France, and two from Turkey. All for employment at the 'Persian Rug Imports.' They were given for six months."

"Isn't it unusual to hire someone from out of the country for only six months?"

"No. Sometimes a new company needs to bring in people with expertise for a while until they can hire help to replace them."

"Thanks, Jim, for the information. By the way, Thursday will work for us to have dinner."

"I will let Kate know. I will see you on Thursday."

I ended the call and went to bed. The next morning, I woke up and checked my phone. Jim Dempsey had sent me a message to call as soon as I could. I sat on the edge of the bed and called him.

"Hello."

"Jim, it's Warren. What's up?"

In an irritated voice, he replied, "Where are you?"

"I'm in southern California visiting my son. Why?'

"What the hell are you getting yourself into?"

"What are you talking about, Jim?"

"Let's not forget I'm with the FBI and have known you for four years. I get a call from you wanting me to run a car license plate. The car is tied to a business in southern California. Then I get flagged that someone is going through state department files looking for work visas for employees brought in to work for that company, and now you tell me you happen to be in southern California. Again, I ask what the hell is going on? Let me remind you going through those files is a crime."

I sat on the edge of the bed, thinking through what to say.

"Jim, I had an uneasy feeling about that car, but let it pass. Then I was sure I was being followed, so I checked out the company. They seemed very suspicious. I had planned to visit my son, so while I was here, I drove by the company, hoping to find information that would put my mind to rest. It only raised my suspicions. Next, I had someone pull in a few favors to get the visa information, which I just received. That's all of it."

There was silence for a long time. Then Jim said, "So, what's your gut feeling, Warren?"

"I think these guys are up to something; for them to travel all the way up north to see what I am up to, it must have something to do with all the shit that went down in Italy."

"What do you plan to do, Warren?"

"Not sure, . . . I think after my visit with my son I will poke around their offices. I will let you know if I turn up anything."

"Be careful, Warren."

"I will be."

I sat there and thought, "I guess I opened that can of worms." I knew Jim would start digging immediately into Persian Rug Imports. I hope I am not putting a small family-owned business under the intense scrutiny of the FBI. I got dressed, made my bed, and headed to the kitchen to have breakfast with the family. After breakfast, we all headed to the zoo.

It was a good weekend. We went to the Getty museum, flew kites at the park at the end of their street, and hung out, enjoying our time together. Monday morning, we all left together. Sally left to take the boys to school, John, to work, and me back to Tustin.

My plane didn't leave until 7:00 in the evening, which gave me most of the day to nose around Persian Rug Imports.

I thought first I would take a chance and go by and talk to the nosey woman neighbor. On Friday, when I drove by, I saw a house for sale just down the street. I pulled up and parked just down the street a short distance from her house. I sat there a moment or two, observing the house of the man I had followed. He didn't appear to be home. I got out and walked to his neighbor's house. Ringing the doorbell, I could hear someone inside approach the door. When the door opened, it was the woman I had seen on Friday.

"Hello, my name is John Scott. My wife and I were thinking of moving to the area, I was wondering if you would answer a few questions about the neighbors. She said sure, then started with her own question. Where did I work, did we have children, did my wife work, on and on she went. The longer we talked, the more comfortable and relaxed she became. It wasn't too long before I got all the information she had on her neighbor across the street without her realizing it. She thought him odd. He kept to himself and had other visitors from time to time, always Middle Eastern men, and never any women. They had him over for a barbeque, but he was distant and would go to great lengths to stay out of any photographs. Finally, I excused myself and left.

I drove over to Persian Rug Imports and parked several blocks away. I walked the several blocks to the office building and concealed myself behind a garbage dumpster and tree at a neighboring building across the street. I was studying the building when two cars pulled up. The person who got out of the first car was about 5' 8" and rather thin, maybe fifty years old. He had a straggly beard and black hair long enough on the sides to cover the ears. He walked briskly to the door, unlocked it, and went in while the two men in the other car were getting out. One was average looking with facial features that were sharp and rather pointed; he reminded me of a rat. Both men had neatly trimmed beards, black hair, about twenty-eight to early thirty years of age. One had a light blue jacket, and the other was wearing a white crochet Kufi Prayer Cap; all three wore jeans.

After about ten minutes, I left my spot, crossed the street, and walked past the two cars parked in the parking lot and continued past the front of the building. There was an alley/driveway between one side of the building and the next building on the street. I turned down the alley with confidence as if I knew where I was going. Just a short way down the alley, there was a high window about eighteen feet up. Must be a window to an office. Looking around, I found an extension ladder near the rear of the building. Placing it against the building carefully to not make a lot of noise, I climbed slowly up and looked in the window. I was right; it was a small office on the second floor. The three of them were standing around a table discussing a building drawing spread out on it. Just then, the rat looked up and saw me. He yelled at the others, and they all headed for the door. I got down as fast as I could and started for the street. In the street, I made a left and started running. They came out the front of the building, saw me and the two younger men started after me. The older man headed for a car.

At my age, there was no way I would outrun them. I crossed the street and made a right at the next street. It was a very short street that you could only go left at the end. There was another alley on my side of the street just as I turned the corner. I quickly turned into the alley. About halfway down the alley was a garbage dumpster. I ran and hid behind it. Looking around, I found a piece of one-inch pipe about twenty-four inches long. There was an alcove for the dumpster, but it was pushed out into the alley for tomorrow's pickup. I stepped back into the alcove to wait.

The two men rounded the corner and one at full speed headed to the end of the street and left. The rat started slowly down the alley with a keen interest in the dumpster and holding a knife at his side. As he looked around the back of the dumpster, I stepped out and nailed him alongside the head. He dropped, knocked out cold. I quickly headed out of the alley and back the way I had come. Finding a place to hide where I could see the street, I waited until dark. The car kept passing by with the one guy for about thirty minutes. Then no more they must have found their friend and had taken him for medical attention.

I made my way back to my car and headed to the airport. I got to the airport, returned the car, and ran with my carryon to check-in. Too late, missed the plane. I sat down in the waiting area and checked my phone for when Maria was arriving. She was arriving tomorrow in San Francisco at 11:45 a.m. I checked flights from John Wayne Airport to San Francisco. There was an Alaska Airlines flight that arrived in San Francisco at 11:10 a.m. Perfect. I walked up to the counter and made the new arrangement. I left the airport and took a taxi to a hotel for the night.

Chapter 48

WAITING AT THE hospital for his man to be released, Anjum was running through different scenarios that would account for the man looking in the window. He wished he would have gotten a better look at the face or had caught him. He couldn't be FBI as they don't peer through windows. Who could it have been? Just then, his man appeared with his head bandaged. They left the emergency room, and on the way to the car, Anjum asked, "Did you get a good look at who did this?"

"No."

When they got back to the office, the rest of the team was there and waiting. There was some concern that the authorities were on to them. Anjum disagreed. Anyone of an official capacity would have men following them for days and would have come to the front door with a warrant, not peering in windows. Then he turned to Fadil and said, "You are sure Warren Steelgrave did not see you following him?"

"I am sure, Anjum."

Anjum didn't believe him. But still, how would Steelgrave know they were associated with Persian Rug Imports. It was more probable that it was one of the business neighbors. The guy that owns the ladder; he could have used it to look into the window, for instance. He had a lot of questions the other day. He was curious as to why, no trucks, and so little activity during the day. It was good; they only have a couple of weeks until the Grammys.

Anjum started the meeting. The bomb had been completed reported Fadal.

"It will be put into a large instrument case and crated up in the next three days. It will be delivered to the staging area for the Grammys next week. The morning of the Grammys and when the bulk of equipment is being delivered into the building. At that time, when they receive word from the men on the loading dock, the power will be shut off for thirty minutes. This will cause the greatest confusion and the best chances to get the bomb uncrated, into the building, and stored under the stage with the rest of the packaging material and instrument cases. We have already hacked into the security system and the electrical grid for that area. All is ready to go."

The rest of the meeting pertained to the positioning of the bomb next to the main column that would bring down the building. Anjum spent an hour going over drawings of the building. Anjum wanted to make sure a well-understood plan was in place to get the bomb from the staging area on the loading dock and to the exact place it needed to be under the main stage. When he was sure there was a clear understanding, he ended the meeting. They would meet once before the Grammys unless something had changed, or a problem arose that had to be taken care of.

After everyone left, Anjum sat in his office thinking, Abir working with the FBI concerned him. He would send a request to headquarters asking them to press the Russians for more information on Abir. There must be a way to put information out that would undermine their trust in him. It was also time to shutdown Persian Rug Imports.

**

Abir sat at his desk, thinking of what Richard might do to discredit him with Zac. He started thinking about what Richard's motives might be. "Was it that Richard thought that he might be a plant or double agent, or was Richard working with the Russians and afraid that because of the intense scrutiny he brought to the division, he might be found out?"

Abir decided it was probably the latter. He decided that everything he did had to be looked at through the filter on how it could be spun in a way to be used against him. He decided to let it go, for now, he had to get his focus back on his work. He logged on his computer and started hardening the internet security for a major utility company on the east coast. This company was under constant cyber-attack. So far, they had only gotten past the first firewalls. He noticed the technique they were using. It was one he had developed. He used his knowledge of how it was being used to follow it back to someone he knew. It was Dabir. He must have escaped as he did when the cell in Italy was taken down.

Abir used his skill and intimate knowledge of Dabir to start tracking his movements on the dark web. He was tired of playing defense; it was time to go on offense and see what is being planned. If he can get information to the director on what was being planned, it would go a long way to build trust between them. He and his family's future depended on how much trust he could build.

Chapter 49

J IM DEMPSEY WAS sitting at his desk when John
Ramsey walked in and took a seat in a chair at the
front of Jim's desk. Jim glanced up, then went back to
reading a document. When he finished reading, he set
the document aside, leaned back in his chair, and said,
"What's up, John."

"I have been checking that company you asked me to
look into, ah . . . Persian Rug Imports. They are very shaky.
I can't find any customers that aren't in cyberspace. They
take orders online wholesale only, and all orders ship from
the Middle East. They paid taxes on two million dollars
profit last year and have eight employees. To me, it looks
like they are laundering money. I think your friend Warren
has stumbled on to something."

Jim became concerned. Why would they travel all the
way north to follow, Warren? What was the connection."

"How long before you can obtain a warrant?"

"We don't have enough now but will keep digging, I will
let you know. This group has been very clever with how
they have set this up."

John got up, and on his way out the door, he said, "I'll let you know as soon as I have more."

After he left, Jim sat there thinking. "It had to be tied to what had happened back in Italy. Why else was Warren being followed in Italy and now again three weeks later."

He picked up his phone and dialed the cyber division of the NSA.

"Hello?"

"Hello, Zac, it's Jim Dempsey. How is Abir working out?"

"Hello, Jim; so far it's been good. I don't think you called to check on, Abir."

"I have a situation I need help with, and I thought Abir might be the answer. The FBI is looking at a company in Tustin, California, that might have a connection to the terrorist cell Abir was connected to. My thought was to fly out and interview him."

"When do you want to come out?"

"I can be there tomorrow?"

"Good, I will see you tomorrow."

Jim hung up the phone and decided to call Warren to see how much more information he might have.

I was sitting in the San Francisco airport waiting for Maria's plane to land when my phone began to buzz. I looked, it was Jim Dempsey calling.

"Hello, Jim, what's up?"

"I wanted to follow up on Persian Rug Imports. The FBI is concerned. After we last talked, we started checking them out. I think you might be right, and there could be a tie between them and the terrorist cell we took down in Italy. Have you thought of anything more about them?"

I went on to tell Jim about my encounter with them the day before and the drawings they were studying.

"I was going to call you later today with my concerns."

"Did you recognize any of them?"

"No, Jim."

Jim thought for a moment, then said, "We will have to stake out the place and get pictures of them and try to associate them to that cell."

"I have an idea, Jim. The leader appears to live across the street from a nosey neighbor, Sandra White, who doesn't trust him, I will send you her address."

We said our goodbyes just as the plane was landing. Jim hung up and then placed an immediate call to the field office in Los Angeles and gave them the address he just received from Warren. The next day, a team turned up to start surveillance on Persian Rug Imports, and another was knocking on the front door of Sandra White. The door opened.

"Hello, may I help you?"

"Mrs. White? We are with the FBI. May we come in?"

She invited them in, and they began their questions. During the questioning, she expressed her concerns about the man across the street.

"He was always so evasive. You could ask him a direct question, and he would answer it for two minutes and really not give an answer. We tried to be good neighbors. We even invited him to a barbeque we had to meet people in the area. He came but got upset when I wanted to take a group photo. It made me really suspicious when he refused to be in the picture, so I did get one when he wasn't looking."

The two agents glanced at each other then, one asked, "Do you still have it?"

"Yes. I have it on my phone."

"Here is my card, would you send it to me right now?"

"Of course."

After receiving the photo, they thanked her for her time and left. Once back in the car, the agent forwarded the photo to Jim Dempsey. Jim's plane was just landing at the private NSA airstrip when he received the photo. There was a car there to pick him up and drive him to the headquarters of the NSA cyber division.

Abir received an email from the director; he wanted to see him in his office. Abir logged off on his computer and headed for the office of the director, all under the watchful eye of Richard. When he walked into director Nohr's office, he was surprised to see Jim Dempsey sitting in front of the director's desk.

"Come in, Abir, you remember Mr. Dempsey from the FBI."

"I do. Good to see you again, Mr. Dempsey."

Jim stood and shook his hand.

"Have a seat, Abir. The FBI needs your help."

Jim turned the chair to the right, away from the front of the desk, and after Abir sat down, he turned his chair to face Jim Dempsey. Jim asked him about the terrorist cell he had been in. Abir didn't know much; all information was compartmentalized. It was done that way, so if someone were caught, they would have only limited information to give up. Then Jim handed him the photo, and as Abir studied it, he began to nod his head slowly and said, "This is Miksa, the brother of Aashiq. He was the leader of our group. I met him only once when he came to meet with as about abducting Mauro Moretti. They were taking me to him in Iran when I escaped."

"Do you have an idea as to why he would be in the United States?"

"They are planning an attack, or he is here to avenge his brother's death, probably both. I have just discovered another member from the cell. He has repeatedly been trying to hack into a power grid on the East Coast. I recognized the technique he was using; I taught it to him. I have been tracking him through the dark web to see if I can find out what they are planning."

Jim looked at Zac with concern, then asked, "Abir, give me your best guess of what you think is happening."

"I was going to come to you, Director, once I was sure. I didn't want to give you information that didn't prove correct. I was afraid you would think I was misdirecting you on purpose. My best guess is that we see so much hacking into companies on the east coast is because they are planning something on the west coast near Miksa."

Zac turned to Abir and said, "Thanks, Abir, you can go back to your office. I will have someone assist you. We need to find out what is being planned."

After Abir left the room, Jim stood and shaking Zac's hand said, "Thanks, Zac, I have to get back and serve a warrant. The FBI jet is waiting for me. I will keep you in the loop with all the information we turn up."

With that, he headed back. From the car, he called John Ramsey so he could start on the warrant. He wanted to serve it on Persian Rug Imports the next day.

Chapter 50

MARIA CAME OUT of the baggage area wearing tan slacks and a deep blue silk blouse. You could not tell she had been on a plane for twelve hours. I walked up to greet her and give her a big hug and kiss. God, she felt good. She stepped back and asked, "Warren, why do you have an overnight bag?"

"Oh, this, I was visiting my son down south and missed my plane yesterday. I flew up from there. Come, let's get an Uber ride and head to the house."

Arriving at the house, I asked if she was hungry. She was a little. I prepared a plate of antipasti, poured two glasses of wine, and we walked out onto the back deck to relax and catch up. I set the food on a small table between two chaise lounge chairs. I sat and laid back watching a large cloud pass overhead against a dark blue sky when she said, "So . . . what kind of trouble have you gotten into while you have been home?"

I wasn't sure how to answer. I didn't want to lie, but I didn't know for sure if I was in trouble or not. I played it off like a joke.

"Not much," I joked.

Maria could tell something wasn't right.

We talked and ate and got caught up with each other's lives. Then Maria's mood changed, and she became more intense.

"Warren, are you going to show me the rest of the house?"

"Of course, Maria."

I stood and took her by the hand to lead her upstairs. My phone buzzed in my pocket; it was Jim Dempsey.

"Hello."

"Warren, I called to let you know I checked out the rug company; you're right: very suspicious. We also sent a couple of agents to the address you gave me to question the neighbor Sandra White. You were right again. She has been keeping an eye on the gentleman across the street from her. He drives the car with the license plate you gave us. She gave us a photo of him she had taken, and our source knows him. His name is Miksa, and he is the brother of Aashiq; I thought you should know. Our source says revenge is a big deal in that culture. We are getting warrants to bring them all in. Until we do, be careful."

"Thanks, Jim."

As they resumed walking upstairs, Maria asked, "FBI, Warren?"

Warren was lost in thought. . . "Ah . . . What?"

"I was standing close enough to catch part of the conversation. I know it was Jim Dempsey. What did he want?"

"He was telling me they were about to arrest the rest of the people that were part of that business in Italy just before the baptism."

I pulled her close and kissed her.

"Maria, I want to take a shower and freshen up."

"I'll join you, Warren."

We got out of the shower and dried each other. I could not hide my excitement as Maria was drying off. She smiled and took my hand. Her eyes were dancing with excitement as she pulled me close and kissed me. She led me to the bed where we made love as if we invented it.

After, she smiled and asked, "What shall we do today, Warren?"

As I was getting up, I turned to her and said, "There is not much of the day left. I could show you around town. I am going downstairs for some water. Do you want me you bring you something?"

"A glass of water would be nice."

I went downstairs and straight to the monitor for the cameras. I looked at the saved video, no strange cars passing the house, or parked on the street for the last two days. I continued to retrieve the water and headed upstairs. As I walked into the bedroom with the water, Maria said,

"Warren, I am tired. Can we eat here and watch a movie? You can show me around tomorrow."

"Of course. I can order food delivered. Do you like Chinese food?"

"I have had it only once."

"I will order Chinese." Throwing her the TV controller, I said, "Find a movie. I will order some food to be delivered, in say two hours."

When I returned, she was still trying to figure out the controller. I laughed and showed her a bottle of wine I had brought upstairs with me; she smiled and nodded yes.

I poured two glasses, and I sat on the bed handing her one; I laid back against the headboard and said,

"I don't want to watch a movie; I want to lie here naked and enjoy your company."

I put on some soft jazz, and we laid there talking about everything under the sun. Finally, Chinese food came. We slipped on robes, went downstairs to receive it, and ate in the kitchen. After we ate, we went back upstairs and laid in bed, watching the news. In about ten minutes, we both were sound asleep in each other's arms.

In the morning, I quietly got up so as not to disturb her and slipped on some sweats and a tee-shirt. I went downstairs, straight to the cameras monitor to examine the tape recording over the last twelve hours. There was nothing unusual recorded. I thought it would be best for us to leave town for a while.

I went into the kitchen and put on the coffee. I next put out some pastries and was cutting up some fruit when Maria appeared wearing my robe.

"I love waking up to the smell of coffee."

I turned and walked over and gave her a kiss and said, "How do you feel?"

"Great. As I get older, the jetlag tires me out in a way it never did before."

I smiled and nodded, I understood. I then poured Maria a cup of coffee. We sat down at the kitchen table and started eating when I said, "Maria, if you are not tired of traveling, I would like to take you up the California coast to a fishing town, Fort Bragg. It's about three and a half hours."

"I would love to; let's go." We quickly cleaned the kitchen, packed our bags, and left. Leaving Hayward, we took highway 580 West over the San Rafael bridge, then north on Highway 101. Entering Fort Bragg, we checked into the North Cliff Hotel, which sits on a bluff high above the ocean.

Entering our room and settling in, Maria walked out onto the balcony to view the ocean and the beautiful late morning day. No fog; warm with a slight chill in the air.

"Warren, come see! The view is spectacular." I walked out onto the balcony and put my arm around her waist. The sun was in a position that framed her in the perfect light with a slight breeze blowing her hair slightly. "God, she is beautiful," I thought.

"What would you like to do for lunch, Maria? We can order room service and eat on the balcony, or just under the bridge where all the fishing boats come in. There are a couple of restaurants there that are very good and have the local fare."

" I am your guest, Warren; surprise me."

"Let's eat under the bridge, then spend the afternoon in Mendocino. If we don't find a better place for dinner, we will come back here, order room service and eat watching the sun slowly set into the ocean." She smiled, and we were off.

There were several restaurants to choose from; we chose "Silver's at The Wharf." We were seated near a large window that looked out to the Noyo river as it met the Pacific Ocean. There were two boats tied to the pier that, for some reason, didn't go out fishing that morning. The setting with the sound of the seagulls, the complex smells of the ocean mixed with smells of the fish made the setting perfect.

As we ate our lunch, I thought through our driving up the 101. I was sure we weren't followed. It would take at least two cars to properly follow us. They wouldn't have had time to put together a team and didn't know where we were going. I had gotten off the freeway twice. Once for gas and once for coffee. No one followed us off the freeway. Now to stay away from the house until the Grammys next week.

Chapter 51

"**D**o you have the warrants, John?"

"I do, Jim. We are all set."

"Good, I am on my way. I will meet you and the team in five minutes."

The plan was that Jim Dempsey would serve the warrant on the business location, and his partner John Ramsey would serve a warrant on the residence across the street from Bob and Sandra White at the same time. After knocking and identifying themselves, both FBI teams entered both locations. Jim immediately took out his phone and called John Ramsey.

"John, anything?"

"No. The place is empty. I have the team going through everything. Dusting for prints, etcetera, and you?"

"The same. I guess seeing Warren Steelgrave looking through the window spooked them. I will meet you back at the office."

Next, Jim called Warren.

Maria and I were just finishing lunch when I got the call. Taking out my phone, I looked at the caller ID.

"What's up, Jim?"

"We came to serve the warrants just now. Everything is as clean as a whistle. You must have spooked them the other day. I thought you should know we haven't picked up anyone I will let you know the moment that changes."

"Thanks, Jim."

I ended the call, and as I was putting away my phone, Maria spoke up, "What's wrong, Warren, you look very concerned?"

I was lost in thought as to what I should do and didn't hear all she had said.

"What? . . . Oh, I am sorry, Maria, I missed what you said."

Maria repeated it.

"That was Jim, letting me know they served the warrants this morning; nothing that concerns us. Let's head to Mendocino. It's not very far, and I think you will enjoy it."

Before I could pay the bill, my phone buzzed again. Taking it out of my pocket, I saw it was Cindy O'Brian. With a kind of puzzled look, I looked at Maria and answered.

"Hello, Cindy. What's up?"

"No. I have asked Maria to attend with me . . . She is with me now. . . Great, that would be nice . . . I'm sure she would like to see you next week . . . Thanks."

I put my phone away, and Maria was looking at me in a not too pleasant way. I knew I had better start explaining.

"Cindy asked if we wanted to attend a few of the parties and events next week. I told her sure."

"Warren, I only brought one dress for the evening of the Grammys."

"I tell you what, Maria; your bag is still packed, right?"

"Yes. We left so quickly I hadn't unpacked at your house; just grabbed it and ran out the door with you."

"I would like a new Tux. Let us do this. We will drive down the coast tomorrow to San Francisco and check into a hotel. We'll have dinner tomorrow night with Jim Marino and his wife. Spend the weekend shopping in San Francisco. Then drive to Los Angeles, spend the week and come back to my place after the Grammys."

"Warren, that would cost a fortune."

"What do I have to spend money on if not you and showing you the time of your life. You will go home having your fill of California. Besides, it's the Grammys. If you weren't here, that is exactly what I would be doing anyway."

She thought for a moment, then smiled and said, "OK. Let's do it."

We left the restaurant and drove to Mendocino. It was a beautiful clear day; warm with a slight coolness in the air. We walked around the village, going into art galleries and handmade designer jewelry shops. In a children's clothing shop, Maria bought some items for her niece and nephew. From the main street, there is a path you can walk out to a bluff that overlooks the Pacific Ocean. We walked out and stood on the edge of the bluff when Maria saw it: a whale passing by.

The sun was getting low in the sky, so we started back to Fort Bragg. We decided to have dinner at the same place where we had lunch. We got there just as the fishing boats were returning for the day. The sky was turning red with the sunset. The boats were in silhouette against it entering the mouth of the river from the Pacific Ocean; it was spectacular. Up the wide river, they came by ones and twos docking at the wharf to unload the days catch.

The next morning, we left right after a small breakfast to drive down the coast on Highway 1 to San Francisco. It was a warm, clear morning, and after a while, Maria asked if we could drive with all the windows down. She wanted to feel the wind in her hair and the smell of the ocean. It would have been the perfect day for a convertible.

Highway 1 follows a lot of the coast high above the ocean. It was slow driving, but the view was fantastic. After about four hours, we came into Bodega Bay for lunch. After lunch, we went on to Petaluma, then on to Sausalito. In Sausalito, we stopped for a coffee.

"Warren, is that San Francisco?

"Yes, Maria, it is. This is one of my favorite views of the city. Let's go; our rooms at the hotel should be ready, and we can freshen up before dinner."

We drove over the Golden Gate Bridge into the city and straight to the Saint Francis Hotel.

"Hope you like this hotel, Maria; it's one of my favorites. We have dinner reservations at the Oak Room tonight at 7:30. Tomorrow we can do some shopping in Union Square. We will stay the night then make our way down the coast to Santa Barbara and finally Los Angeles."

We checked into our room on the thirty-second floor. I was looking out the window, enjoying the view when Maria walked up behind me and slid an arm around my waist and put her head on my shoulder. We looked out over the city and Union Square with the cable cars clanking and ringing their bells as they went up and down Powell street in front of the hotel.

"Warren, the view is something. What a beautiful city."

"I thought you would like it. Let me get ready for dinner."

We went down to the Oak Room in the hotel. When we got there, Jim and his wife Kate had just arrived and were waiting for the hostess to return. I walked up and tapped Jim on the shoulder. When he turned, I said, "Perfect timing. Jim and Kate, you remember, Maria?"

Kate spoke up. "Of course! How have you been, Maria? And your dad?"

"I have been good, Kate, and my dad is doing as well as can be expected. Thank you for asking."

We were seated and ordered martinis. After a few minutes, Maria and Kate excused themselves to go to the lady's room. Jim waited until they were gone then asked me, "What's going on with the guys in Los Angeles?"

"One of them is the brother of Aashiq. Do you remember him? He was leading the group that was taken down in Italy last spring. The FBI is concerned they are in Los Angeles to pull off an attack and are trying to arrest them. Before they could serve the arrest warrants, they all have gone underground."

"And you, Warren?"

"I have gone underground also until they are caught. Tomorrow we leave for Los Angeles until after the Grammys. By then, they should be in custody."

"Anything you need me to do, Warren?"

"No. I think the FBI will have them in a few days."

Just then, Maria and Kate returned. We all had a great time at dinner.

The next day after breakfast in bed, Maria and I left for a day of shopping in and around Union Square. First, we shopped for the things we knew would need tailoring. Two dresses for her a new tuxedo for me. All were guaranteed to be delivered to the hotel by 5:00 that evening. Then to Gumps for accessories. After an exhausting day, we returned to the hotel to find the new garments hanging in the closest. Trying them on, all fit. It was the most fun Maria had had in a long, long time.

The next morning, we left early without breakfast. We would eat somewhere along the coast on our way to Santa Barbara. A day and night in Santa Barbara, then on to Los Angeles.

Chapter 52

ANJUM HAD ARRIVED at a restaurant near Thousand Oaks, California, for a meeting with Miksa. Everyone had moved out of Tustin and scattered to towns outside the Los Angeles area. Anjum was meeting with Miksa to go over the final plans.

After being seated at a table in the rear of the restaurant, Anjum started the conversation.

"Miksa, let me ask you about this Warren Steelgrave. Do you think he was the one that informed the FBI?"

"I don't know. I don't think so. I sent two men north to his home to pick him up, as you asked. When they got there, he was not home. A neighbor was walking her dog; they asked her when she thought he would return; they wanted to meet with him over a possible movie deal on one of his books. She said she didn't know that he had left with a woman and suitcases the day before and asked that she pick up and hold his mail for several weeks."

Anjum thought for a moment then went on.

"I guess it doesn't matter, everything is in place. They got the bomb through security this morning. No one on the team has been picked up. If Abir was the one who let the FBI know we are planning something, they don't know when or where. If they knew, the bomb would have never gotten through security. Still, they must be looking really hard . . . Let's do this. Let's put some chatter on the internet about something going to happen at this weekend's NFL football game. Let us keep our team out of the chatter, maybe between headquarters and someone in Paris. We are only one day away; this will give them something to focus on."

"Let's go through the sequence for detonating the device, Miksa."

"First would be to use a coded signal sent over the Wi-Fi; if for some reason that is detected and fails, we will use a cell phone. The last option would be to send in one of the roadies and detonate it by hand. The largest viewer audience is at the end of the show during the announcing of the song of the year. They break for a commercial just before the announcement. When they come back from the commercial, a signal is sent, letting the producer know they are again live on air. It's this signal that will detonate the bomb. If that fails, I will detonate it with a cell phone. If by the end of announcing the winner, it hasn't gone off, our man will make his way to under the stage and detonate it by hand."

Anjum sat there, going through the whole scenario in his mind looking for any missed detail. Finally, after he was satisfied nothing had been missed, he looked at Miksa and said,

"OK. Tell everyone to stay out of sight until after. I do not want anyone picked up trying to leave the country early; understood?"

Miksa shook his head slightly up and down, acknowledging he understood. They finished dinner and left.

***

Abir was seated at his desk when he noticed some unusual internet traffic on the dark web. He sent an email to the director, asking to see him. He got an immediate response to come upstairs.

Abir found the director's door open and was motioned by the director to come in.

"Thanks for seeing me, Director. I have printed out the following from the dark web."

He handed three sheets of the printout to the director keeping three copies for himself. Continuing, he went on, "Sir, I have highlighted the terms and language that are important. They are planning something big in the Los Angeles area this weekend. I am afraid if I keep checking and find it, the mole will let them know we are on to them. The information so far points to something happening this weekend at the NFL football game. I think that is a ruse. I know these guys. I would bet they went underground, have the plan in motion, and are staying off the internet."

Zac leaned back in his chair and thought for a moment, then picked up the phone and placed a call to Jim Dempsey.

"Jim, it's Zac. What's happening out there?"

"Hello, Zac. We are trying to find these guys, but by the time we got warrants, they disappeared. We are still looking, but Los Angeles is a big place."

"Abir just came in and predicted they would go underground. He says that is because they have a plan in motion. I will get back to you as soon we have a plan of our own."

Ending the call, Zac asked Abir what he suggested we do.

"Sir, I know I am under constant surveillance in several different ways. This makes it easy for the mole to monitor what I am doing. If I am right and something is about to be attacked, it is of extreme importance to them to keep an eye on me. If you would trust me and remove all surveillance on me, the mole will have to notify them. If the right kind of trap is set, the mole will send word I am off the grid, and we will have him. Trust me, I will find the target."

"Abir, how long will it take you to set the trap?"

"I bet you have it in place already trying to find the mole. The problem is there is so much surveillance trying to trap me. Once the surveillance is removed from me, and you are only looking for one, it should be quick."

"Sit tight. I will be right back."

Zac was gone about an hour, and on his return, he sat in the second chair in front of his desk. Turning the chair to face Abir, he began.

"Here is what has been decided, Abir. You are taking a plane out to Los Angeles. Jim Dempsey will pick you up. You were right; we do already have a trap in place. After you are in the air, all surveillance on you will be dropped. You will be missed, and we will watch the trap. Once you are in Los Angeles, you will work out of the FBI office. Once you have identified the target because you know Miksa by sight and maybe a few others, you will join Jim Dempsey's team in the field. Our goal is to take down this cell before they can execute their plan. Any questions?"

Abir shook his head no.

"Good."

They both stood, and Zac shook Abir's hand and said, "You need to leave now. I will brief your wife."

Abir stood and was escorted out of the building to a waiting car that would take him to the plane. Abir knew this was his one shot to prove himself loyal to the country. He vowed to himself he would not fail.

Chapter 53

MARIA AND I ARRIVED in Los Angeles on Monday and checked into the Beverly Hilton. The first few days, we toured the usual tourist sites. Tonight was the first of the Grammy Parties we were invited to. We decided to lay around the pool most of the day. Later in the afternoon, Maria had an appointment at the spa. While she was at the spa, I decided I would get a haircut. I went to make an appointment with the hotel barber. The barbershop was booked solid. Having several hours to kill, I decided to go downtown to find a barbershop. Driving down Sunset Blvd. I stopped and parked a few doors down from a neighborhood barbershop that looked like it could use some business. I got out and walked in.

"Good afternoon, is it possible to get a trim?"

"Of course, I accept walk-ins."

After I finished getting my haircut, I still had an hour to kill. I decided I would go by the Grammy Museum where the party was going to be held. As I drove past the museum, I saw him. He was coming out of the museum looking around as I passed by. I found a place to park and called Jim Dempsey.

"What, Warren?"

"Jim, I am just south of the Grammy Museum and as I passed by coming out of the Museum was, ah . . . the guy . . . the guy you identified as . . . damn, I can't think of his name."

"Warren, do you mean, Miksa?"

"Right, Miksa."

"Thanks, Warren, we will send a team by right away."

I decided to drive around a little to see if I could find him and see where he went. I couldn't find him and decided to go back to the hotel.

Jim Dempsey was waiting for Abir's plane to land when he got the call from Warren. When Abir got into the car, Jim told him about the call, "Abir, do you think the party tonight at the museum will be the target?"

Abir was quiet, thinking through everything, then responded, "No, I think something bigger. Get me on a computer, so I can get to work. I will find the target."

***

I was in our room sitting at a small table in front of a window with a glass of white wine looking out over the pool; when Maria walked in.

"You got a haircut, Warren! I like it."

She walked over, poured herself a glass of wine, and sat down.

"How was the spa, Maria?"

"Fantastic, Warren."

"Shall we get ready and head over to the party?"

She smiled and nodded, yes. I could feel her excitement. I thought, "I hope all goes well tonight."

Our taxi delivered us to the front of the museum about fifteen minutes after the official start. We got out and walked over to the VIP line to have our invitations and ID's checked. We were in line about five back from Elton John. I could feel the excitement in Maria. We walked into the museum and started viewing the displays when we were each handed a glass of champagne. I looked over, and near the Michael Jackson display, Cindy was having her picture taken by a few of the press. She looked up, and our eyes met. She smiled, and the connection was as strong as ever. Maria squeezed my hand so hard I thought she would break a small bone.

Within seconds, Cindy's manager whisked her away for a group photo with the other nominees. It was going to be a very busy night for Cindy with little contact with anyone other than promoters and press. We walked around with our drinks star-struck. We would come upon tables of food, and our glasses were kept full. After a couple of hours, Maria had had enough, and we left to go back to the hotel.

We ordered a glass of wine from the bar and found a quiet spot near the pool to sit. It was a warm night with no one in the pool area but us. We sat quietly until Maria finally broke the silence.

"Cindy still loves you a lot, Warren."

I didn't know how to respond. I took a sip of my wine and just sat there.

"Warren, can we not go to another party. I enjoyed tonight . . . but once is enough."

"I was hoping you would say that. We will find a romantic place for dinner tomorrow night. Maria . . . I hope you don't take this wrong, but I am here with you, and I don't want to hear anything about Cindy. It's early, let's go to bed and find a movie."

Maria smiled, "OK, Warren."

***

Miksa walked out of the Grammy Museum as they were closing to get ready for the party in honor of this year's Grammy nominations. He had grabbed a flyer on the way out. That afternoon in his room, reading the list of nominees, he saw the name Cindy O'Brian: Warren's girlfriend. He went back that evening just before the start of the party and waited across the street as people arrived. Just as he thought, Warren Steelgrave was attending the party. He smiled, knowing Warren Steelgrave would also be at the Grammy Awards. If he survived the bomb blast, Miksa would be waiting to kill him in the chaos that followed. He would have one of the men working that night get Warren Steelgrave's assigned seat number for him.

Chapter 54

ABIR WAS GIVEN a small private office to work in the FBI office building. It was next to Jim Dempsey's office and had no windows and plain white walls. There was a desk, a computer with a printer, and a straight back wooden chair. He sat down at the computer and went straight to work. Again, he was finding little bits of information that put together indicated the NFL game was the target. He didn't buy it. He was finding the information too easily. Abir sat back and began to think through what he did know. It was going to be this weekend for sure. He did a Google search of events this weekend. He was amazed at the number of things happening in the Los Angeles area over the weekend.

The NFL game and the Grammys would have the biggest crowds. Knowing Miksa and how they had been trained to think, he was sure they were leaving clues to lead him to believe the NFL game was the target. He decided to put his focus on the Grammys.

He began searching on the dark web for information. Looking for anything involving anyone he knew from the past. After hours of searching: Nothing. Of course, they have gone silent because they know he is searching. All is in place, and the plan has been executed and will run to completion without further communication. Then he got an idea. All the information gathered from the internet is stored someplace. He got up and went next door to Jim Dempsey's office. Jim was sitting at his desk.

"Excuse me, Inspector, I need some information."

"Want kind of Information, Abir?'

"I need all the internet traffic going back for two months."

" Do you realize the volume of the information you are requesting?"

"Yes, but we can narrow it to information originating from the Los Angeles area."

Jim nodded and said it would be delivered to his computer shortly. Abir left the office and walked down the hall to the coffee machine for a cup of coffee. When he returned to his office, a password-protected file was in his computer's inbox.

He opened the file and started carefully reading through the information. Then he found it. Last month, a message went out from the server at Persian Rug Imports. It was coded and sent to eight people in a group sending. It was about a plan to be executed in the evening and on the same date as the Grammys, which was tonight. Abir knew he could be wrong; if he was and the attack happened somewhere else, his life would be over. He would be thought of as someone planted to give false information to be used as a diversion. He could play it safe and wait until he was sure, but there was no time for that. He had to try to prevent this attack. He headed back to Jim's office. Walking in, he laid a printout of what he had found on Jim's desk.

"Inspector, I believe the target is the Grammys tonight."

Jim knew that a shitstorm would erupt if he tried to cancel the Grammys. What if Abir was wrong and the Grammys were canceled; he could not imagine the fallout and the careers ruined, starting with his.

"How sure are you, Abir?"

"I am pretty sure, sir."

"Pretty sure isn't enough. Keep looking, I will get started on what has to be done."

"I will need some help, sir."

"I will have someone to help you in about ten minutes."

Abir went back to his office and started searching for more information. A second desk and chair were brought in. In just a few minutes, a woman appeared with her laptop computer.

"Hello, Abir, I am special agent Jane Simmons I am here to help; what do you want me to do?"

Abir showed her where he was and how he wanted to proceed. He had identified the server and a sent group of emails. He needed her to help find all the other emails in the traffic between the group. It wasn't long before he was decoding emails; there were hundreds over the past two months.

Jim was meeting with his top people. The Grammys were already a top priority, and the security was very high all week. Jim explained that because the group had gone silent, Abir felt security and been breached, and the plan is proceeding on its own without any more communication needed between them. Then Jim was asked if he trusted the information given by Abir. Jim answered that he did. Jim knew with that statement he had sealed his fate with that of Abir.

Abir looked up from what he was doing and saw Jane focused intently on something.

"What, Jane?"

I have run across this email that is different than the rest. It was received by the main server then forwarded on to someone not on the list you gave me."

Abir got up and walked over to look at it. Reading the message in Arabic, he realized the importance of it. Miksa had received a message which read: "The delivery was made today; all is good." It was supposed to look like it was about a shipment of rugs being delivered. The fact that it was forwarded to someone in Iran and the group went silent after. It had no order number, or customer name like other emails could only mean a bomb was delivered safely through security to the Grammys. Abir immediately went to Jim with the information. Jim thanked Abir and put in motion a plan to hunt down the bomb. He had men already there undercover with devices that could sniff the air looking for a bomb. The problem was that Grammys had already started.

Abir said he would go back and search for more information; with some luck, he could uncover the rest of the plan. Abir left to go back to work. Jim realized Warren and Maria were at the Grammys with tickets provided by Cindy. He took out his phone and sent a text message to Warren. "Leave now! There is a bomb at the Grammys: the terrorist target."

Chapter 55

I WAS SITTING AT the table with a martini I had made myself from the minibar waiting for Maria to finishing dressing. She emerged from the bedroom in a long black evening gown with black heels. She had a hand-embroidered evening wrap. It was a dark maroon background of batik silk with an embroidered garden of flowers. It was stunning. I was just at that time, taking a sip of my martini when she walked out, and the shock caused me to spill some on my new tuxedo. With a playful little laugh, she said, "Warren, are you OK?"

I set down the drink and grabbed a napkin to wipe up that which spilled.

"I am fine, Maria, you look stunning."

She took off the wrap revealing a strand of opera length pearls, which were some of the largest matched pearls I have ever seen. A four-row diamond tennis bracelet with hanging earrings that matched. Holding the wrap over one arm, she slowly made a full circle.

"What do you think, Warren. Is the wrap a little too bright?"

"Not at all, Maria."

I finished my drink and walked over to her and gave her a hug and kiss. I love the fact that she wears very little makeup, and I can do that without lipstick and makeup on my collar or her complaining I am messing up her face. I pulled back a little and smiling, asked, "Shall we go?"

She nodded yes; I took her by the hand, and we were off to the Grammys.

I had ordered a driver and a large black Mercedes sedan for the evening. We arrived, and our driver got in line with the limousines. After a few minutes, security checked the car and inspected our driver's licenses with the names on the tickets. Then we were passed through to the line of limousines delivering people to the red carpet. Our doors were opened, and a gentleman on each side of the car helped us out. The gentleman who helped Maria get out of the car stood with her while I came around from the other side and joined them. With a slight tilt of the head, he handed me Maria's arm and addressed us.

"Have a wonderful evening."

With that, we were on our way down the red carpet at the Grammys. There were celebrities in front of us and behind us. Some were pulled aside for interviews. I have to admit, not too much impresses me, but this was the coolest thing I have ever done.

We walked in, and with some help, we found our assigned seats. I felt my hand being squeezed. I looked at Maria, who was smiling. She then leaned forward and whispered, "What a fairytale; this is unbelievable."

Just then, the house lights faded out, and the program began. About two-thirds through my phone buzzed. I took it out and saw I had received a message from Jim Dempsey. "Leave now! There is a bomb at the Grammys: the terrorist target." The blood drained from my face. At two-thirds through the program, it could go off any minute. I took Maria by the hand and stood. She looked puzzled but stood and followed me out of the row to the aisle, then to the outside of the building. I called our driver and told him to pick us up in front. Maria could feel my urgency and kept asking what's wrong. After calling our ride, I turned to her and said, "Maria, I got a text from Jim of the FBI. There is a bomb at the Grammys. When the car gets here, go back to the hotel. I will meet you there later."

"Later! Where are you going?"

"I have to find Cindy and warn her."

Maria grabbed my arm and hung on. Her eyes were begging me to not go back in. I just shook my head, removed her grip on my arm, and headed back into the building.

Where to go to find Cindy. I saw Garth Brooks get out of his seat and come up the aisle. He was being given directions to make his way to the back of the stage. I remember he was one of the presenters. I started to follow him; I didn't get very far before I was stopped by security. Luckily for me, she was FBI and recognized me.

"Mr. Steelgrave, I have been looking for you. Jim Dempsey was afraid you might not have gotten his text."

"I got it. You and I have to get to Cindy O'Brian backstage and let her know."

"Mr. Steelgrave, I can't let you go back there."

I pulled out my phone.

"Do you want me to call Jim and tell him you are detaining me? He's quite busy right now."

She hesitated and thought for a moment. For Warren to have been sent a text from her boss and her given orders to find him gave him some importance; she wasn't sure how much. She had seen the text, and maybe he was asked to do something, she had decided.

"Follow me, I will take you to her."

Abir had figured it out and was almost in a panic when he burst into Jim's office and blurted out. "The bomb will detonate after the last commercial."

Jim looked at his watch; they had fifteen minutes.

"Do you know how they plan to do it, Abir?"

"Yes. When the last commercial airs, it sends a signal to the producer giving him a ten-second countdown to go on air, which triggers the bomb. My guess is the bomb detonates sometime later, maybe thirty seconds, making sure they are on the air when it explodes. They always have a backup, in this case, I would bet a signal from a cell phone."

"Can you block the cell signal?"

Abir thought a minute, then answered, "No. It would take to long to isolate that one phone. What I can do with Mauro's protocol is to shut down all cell phone service in the Western United States."

"Well get it in place, I will give the signal when it should go down."

Jim then called special agent John Ramsey in the field at the Grammys. He explained the situation and instructed him to get all in charge of the broadcast; tell them that they were not to go to any commercials. John was to start an orderly evacuation of everyone, starting with the nonessential personal. They need to speed up the broadcast and end early. Then evacuate the building as quickly as possible.

"What kind of progress has the bomb squad made, John?"

"Almost sixty percent of the building."

"Good. Keep me posted, I will be cutting off all cell phone and radio transmission as soon as we can. I will be on my way over as soon as we do."

"Got it. I will take care of this end."

***

I was taken back to the area where the performers and presenters gathered, waiting to be told it was their turn to step out onto the stage. The FBI and local police were evacuating everyone who had finished their appearances and all nonessential personnel needed to finish the broadcast.

I found Cindy and walked up to her. She was in conversation with someone about the confusion spreading as people were ushered out emergency exits. Everyone was checking their cell phones trying to call and get information on what was happening: none were working. I walked up and touched her arm; she turned, startled. When she saw it was me, she became concerned.

"Warren, what are you doing here?"

"I haven't time to explain. You have to get out now!"

"I am not leaving; they are about to announce the awards for best song of the year."

I took her by the arm and led her away from everyone.

"Cindy, there is a bomb planted somewhere. It could go off any minute, you have to leave."

"Warren, I am not leaving until they announce the winner, and if I should win, I am walking out there to receive my award. This is my life's dream. Better to die here than in the future dying of cancer wishing I had stayed."

It was said with such determination I knew there was no talking her out of it. It was no different than Maria begging me to leave with her and not go back into the building.

"Fine, I will stay with you. I feel the same, I would rather die here with you then some future date with cancer."

The last performer was just finishing. This was where they would go to commercial; they hadn't had a commercial for the last half hour. Authorities were starting to evacuate the live audience off camera. They would announce the winner of the song of the year and close the show.

***

Miksa was watching the broadcast on television in his room several blocks away. He could tell something was wrong. He took out his cell phone to call Abbud: it was dead. He knew instinctively Abir had discovered the plan. He put on his shoes and left to make his way over to the hall. He had to get word to Abbud to detonate the bomb by hand. Before he reached the hall, he saw Abbud coming his way.

"Abbud, where are you going?"

"Miksa, we have to leave, the place is crawling with FBI."

"But the bomb?"

Abbud smiled. "Tarif is on his way to detonate it. He was working as a stagehand: when everyone got word, there would be no more commercials he called me. He was on his way to detonate it when, in the middle of our conversation, the cell phone quit working. Let's get out of here."

Chapter 56

I WAS WAITING NERVOUSLY near where Cindy was standing with the other four nominees. All four were nervous, waiting for the announcement of the winner. Then I saw him open a stage door, and just before going through it, he looked around. His eyes and mine met; it was the rat, the one I knocked out in the alley. He went through the door. I made my way across the area and through the door right behind him.

The other side of the door led to a passageway and stairs going down under the stage. I got to the bottom of the stairs and looked around. The area was large and was dimly lit with long dark shadows. It had the smell of musty, stale air. I stood a moment allowing my eyes to adjust. The area was crowded with crates and instrument cases of all sizes. I heard a noise close by and headed toward it. Then I saw him; he had been moving a large crate that had been placed next to a large instrument case. Having moved the crate to expose enough space to open the instrument case, he was bent over unlatching it. The bomb, I thought.

I ran over to him and grabbed his left arm. He rose up, and as he turned trying to steady himself, I delivered a right cross to the head. He wobbled, trying to keep his balance but tripped over something on the floor and fell. Pulling up a pant leg, he pulls out of a scabbard a large knife. Determined to keep him away from the bomb until help arrived, I looked around for something to defend myself with.

The only thing immediately in reach was a metal folding chair. "Oh, great," I thought. Grabbing the chair and holding it with both hands, I waited for him to come at me. I used a quick thrusting motion with the chair to hold him at bay. Finally, I timed it just right; as he lunged for the chair, I thrust a leg of the chair into his gut. The pain and response to grab the chair caused him to drop the knife. We both let go of the chair, and he made a move to pick up the knife. I came up with a knee and broke his nose. Just then John Ramsey and the bomb squad arrived John was putting handcuffs on the rat. When the guy from the bomb squad said, "You better get out of here; this has been triggered, and the clock is running."

John and I looked over and saw that the guy from the bomb squad had opened the case and was looking at a flashing red light and the LED clock counting down.

"How much time?" John asked.

Still studying the bomb with a deep focus, he responded.

"The clock says thirty minutes, but I am not sure I would want to trust that. This is the final backup. At a set time, it armed itself and started the countdown. If no one got to it to detonate, it would detonate itself. Make sure everyone is out of the building then I will try to disarm it. It looks like it is going to be simple, but who knows."

John and I headed up the stairs. The broadcast had concluded, and the building was almost empty. We walked out onto the loading dock, and several more of the bomb team was headed into the building with the bomb containment unit on a large motorized cart. Once inside near the door that led to under the stage, two men would carry the bomb up the stairs and place it into the unit. John and I were the last to have made it out to the street. Five minutes later, the containment unit was placed on a truck; with a police escort, it was headed out of the city. I looked at my watch; they still had fifteen minutes to get to a detonation site.

None of the television viewers had any idea of what had happened, only that the show ended early this year instead of running long. As I stood watching the truck rush off with the bomb, I felt a hand slide down the inside of my arm and grasp my hand. I turned it was Cindy. I turned and said, "Well, did you win?"

With a tilt of the head and shrug of her shoulders, she answered, "No."

"I am sorry, Cindy; there is always next year."

She pulled me close and hugged me tightly. After a few moments, we separated, and I looked at her and said, "Still a Grammy nomination is quite an accomplishment. Thank you for allowing me to be part of it."

Just then, her manager came up and said, "Cindy, they want pictures of all the nominees. The photographer is waiting."

As her manager pulled on Cindy's arm, she resisted a moment. Cindy and I just stared at each other; then, she was gone. Just then, Jim Dempsey walked up with special agent John Roberts. Jim stuck out his hand and shook mine.

"John tells me we were lucky tonight you saved the day, keeping the terrorist from detonating the bomb."

I was inspecting several tears in my new tuxedo when I answered, "Nothing heroic; I just didn't want to be blown up is all. Do you think I can get reimbursed for my tuxedo?"

Jim laughed. "No. We don't even get reimbursed for clothing."

"How about a ride to my hotel? My cell phone isn't working."

"That I can do."

As they were walking to Jim's car, they were being watched. Miksa was standing across the street in the rapidly dispersing crowd. "Steelgrave always Steelgrave," he thought. "If I don't get him before, I will get him when he returns home."

They got to the hotel, and I said goodnight and went straight upstairs to find Maria. When I got to the room, she had changed clothes and was packed.

"Warren, I was just leaving you a note. I wasn't sure what time you might get back. I have booked myself a flight home on a late evening flight."

I started to say something, but she stopped me.

"You love her so much you were willing to die with her." She tilted her head a little and continued, "I don't want to say something I will regret. Tomorrow and maybe the next day you will be busy with the FBI and press. We will talk after everything has settled down a little. OK?"

I just nodded, yes. Maria walked up to me and gave me a heartfelt hug and left. I made myself a martini from the minibar and sat at the table overlooking the pool to think. "What is my life becoming, but a series of relationships separated by long stretches of being totally alone. Not as bad as it sounds. People are complicated; maybe being alone is not all bad." I smiled, finished my drink, and went to bed.

Chapter 57

I AWOKE TO THE sound of my phone buzzing. I grabbed it; it was Jim Marino.

"Hello."

"Warren, what the hell is going on. Are you OK? How about Maria and Cindy, they OK? The papers this morning said the Grammy show ended early because of a bomb scare."

"We are all fine. The FBI has one suspect in custody and is rounding up the rest of the people involved as we speak. Maria has headed home, and I am about to do the same. I will call you when I get there, and we can go to lunch. I will fill you in on the details then."

Next, my daughter Sherry called; I told her the same as I told Jim. Then the phone buzzed again; it was Jim Dempsey.

"Good morning, Jim."

"Good morning, Warren. How soon can you come by the office for a formal statement?"

"Give me an hour to dress, pack, and check out."

"OK. See you when you get here."

I showered and packed. As I was leaving the room, I thought to myself, "Heard from everyone except Cindy."

I arrived at the FBI offices close to 10:30. I was taken to a small office and given a pen and pad to write out my statement. It took me a little over an hour. Just as I was finishing, Jim walked in.

"All done, Warren?"

"Just finishing."

"Good. Let's go to lunch while it's typed up. You can sign it when we return. There's someone I want you to meet."

We got to the lobby, and a gentleman was waiting for us.

"Warren, I would like you to meet Abir Sadiq. He is responsible for killing all cell phones and jamming the detonation of the bomb as well as identifying the target."

"Glad to meet you, Abir. Let me shake your hand and say thank you. You saved a lot of lives last night, including my own."

After lunch, we went back to the FBI offices. I read over my statement, signed it, and left for home. I would stop at my son's for the night and continue home tomorrow. Abir walked out with me to catch a plane back to Virginia. He stopped me in front of the building and said, "Mr. Steelgrave, I was in the cell that had abducted Mauro Moretti. I am so glad he is alive; it was his protocol that allowed me to hack into and shut down all the cell phones so quickly. If you get a chance, please tell him."

Then he gave a brief account of how he ended up working for the United States. We said our goodbyes, and as we shook hands, he said, "Be careful, Mr. Steelgrave. Miksa will continue to come after you until one of you are dead.

Because of last night's failure, he is a dead man and cannot go home. This makes him very dangerous."

I nodded my head, I understood, and we left walking in different directions.

As I started driving to my son's house, my mind drifted through the events of yesterday, then to Abir's words of caution. "I knew he was right and that Miksa knew where I lived. Time was on his side; I was the one playing defense. I would have to find a place to stay that gave me a little advantage: but where?"

***

Abir leaned back in his seat as the plane took off, he thought about his wife and what would happen on his return. He wondered if they caught the mole and if it was Richard. Because of the success of yesterday, Richard would have to curtail any efforts to set him up. He fell asleep and woke up as they were landing. It was almost 11:00 p.m. when he got home. His wife was excited to see him.

"Where are the children?"

"In bed, they stayed up as long as they could; they stayed up late last night watching the Grammys. Knowing you were there, they watched late into the morning, hoping to hear more details. They were exhausted today. Finally, around 10:00 tonight, I found them asleep on the couch and made them go to bed. Let's go to bed. I want all the details, my husband."

The next morning, Abir drove to work. When he got to his office, it was empty except for Richard. When he walked in, Richard walked up to him reaching to shake his hand.

"Great job, Abir. My wife's sister was at the Grammys last night. I cannot tell you how grateful the family is. The director wants me to bring you to his office."

Abir was a little stunned but followed Richard to the elevator and up to the director's office. When they walked in, Abir froze. The office was full of people standing; many he did not know. They were all clapping and in front were his wife and daughters. She had come here with them instead of school. Director Zac Nohr stepped up and shaking his hand said, "Job well done, Abir. The country thanks you."

After a while, everyone started getting back to work. Abir's wife left to get the girls to school. Abir was still a little dazed when the director asked him to take a seat.

"Abir, because of the secrecy of our work, there will be no public acknowledgment of your accomplishment. But the State Department is going to give you and your wife green cards giving you legal status and the ability to become naturalized citizens in the future."

They stood, and as Abir started to leave, Zac said, "By the way, the trap caught the mole. You were right. After we dropped the surveillance on you, within minutes, she tried to get the word out that you were headed to Los Angeles. It was Doris in the cubical next to yours."

Abir nodded, and on his way back to his office, looked up to heaven and said thank you.

Chapter 58

I SPENT THE NIGHT at my son's house. He and his wife wanted all the details. I left out the details about my fight with the terrorist, and my involvement with the FBI. Just the details of being at the Grammys and Cindy's performance, etcetera. I was about halfway home when my phone buzzed: Cindy. Before I could hit the reject call button, the car answered, "Hello, Cindy."

"Hello, Warren, do you have a minute?"

"Yes, I am alone."

"Where's Maria?"

"She has left to go home to Italy. I am driving back to Hayward."

"I wanted to call sooner but didn't want to add to the drama. I wasn't sure how Maria had taken being in the middle of a bomb scare . . . I would love to see you; maybe dinner at your house?"

"Where is Rick?"

"He left on a fishing trip with Ben. I fly home tonight."

I thought for a few minutes, then responded, "Cindy, I won't be able to for a while. I have some loose ends with all this bombing business I have to tend to."

"What kind of loose ends?"

I didn't answer. The truth be told, I wasn't sure I wanted to see Cindy. I have had my own significant emotional event almost being killed and wasn't sure how I felt about any of the current relationships. Her or Maria. I needed some time alone.

"I understand. Call me when you have things settled. I love you."

"*Anche me.*"

I disconnected the call. Then I started looking for a car following me. I was on highway five, headed north, and at times, there can be little traffic. Every time a car started to pass, I prepared myself to defend against being run off the road and shot.

I arrived home just after 6:00 p.m., unpacked, and headed for the bar and a martini. I sat in the living room and started thinking about Abir. Several months back, he was the enemy, doing what he could to help bring down my way of life and me. Then two days ago, he saved it. He was part of the group that abducted Mauro; now wants me to get word to Mauro that it was his protocol that saved the lives of many. I started a serious relationship with Maria, and Cindy is back in my life. How strange life can be. How strange relationships are and how complicated and troublesome they can be. Then it came to me: Mendocino. It often happens to me; when I have a problem that I am struggling with looking for an answer if I let my mind sort of free think an answer just pops up.

I will leave early tomorrow morning. Mendocino is small enough I will be able to set a trap for Miksa. I will leave enough clues that it will be easy to find out where

I am. I have been there many times over the years and know it like the back of my hand.

The next morning, I left the house early, and as I made a left onto the street that leads into Hayward. I saw an empty blue Ford parked on the street. I made my way through town and onto the freeway 580 West. After crossing the San Rafael bridge, I headed north on highway 101. I was coming to Santa Rosa, and I decided to see if the blue Ford had followed me. I took an off-ramp and stopped for gas. I got back on the freeway and paid close attention to the next on-ramp. Sure, enough parked on the side of the on-ramp about halfway down was a blue Ford. After he saw me pass, he got back on about three cars back. I purposely left the car out of the garage last night, so it would be easy for him to attach a tracking device to the car. I wasn't sure he was waiting in Hayward when I got home, but I am now. What I have to do is lead him to where I want to spring the trap.

I came into Mendocino and parked in front of the Mendocino Hotel. The hotel was opened in 1878 and, in its history, had been a bordello. It is located on Main Street with views of the ocean. It is a great Victorian hotel furnished with period furnishings. I went in and on check-in requested a room with a view of the ocean. I went up to my room and put my overnight bag on the brass bed. I walked over and opened the door to the small balcony and walked out. What a view of the ocean, but more important was the vantage point to view all of Main Street. I looked down Main Street, and there it was parked, a blue Ford: perfect.

Taking a roll of quarters out of my overnight bag, I went down to the restaurant and ordered dinner. After dinner,

I put a linen napkin in my coat pocket, paid the tab, and headed outside for a walk. This time of night, there was no one on the street. I figured he would not want to use a gun, knowing it would be just too loud. He would want to catch me on one of the smaller streets to do the deed with a knife. I needed him to follow me down an alley. Where was he? I went into an art gallery that was just about to close. When I came out, I looked up and down the street. I saw just the bill of a baseball cap protruding out from a doorway. I turned and started down the street the opposite way. I turned left on the next street and saw an alley two blocks down on the same side of the street; I turned down it. It was a pass-through to another street. It was dark and damp lit only by one small light mounted halfway down the alley from the side of the building. If I were being followed, he would turn down this alley; not seeing me would pick up the pace, maybe even begin to run to the end of the alley so as not to lose me on the next street. I had to be ready to act quickly. I found a deep doorway just inside the alley to conceal myself.

I reached into my coat pocket and grasped the roll of quarters. Taking them out, I wrapped my hand with the linen napkin. I wouldn't want to break my hand when I hit this guy. Just then, he turned into the alley and stopped just before the doorway. I could tell it was Miksa.

He paused a second then started to run to the end of the alley. As he passed the doorway, I pushed him and he lost his balance. As he was stumbling trying to recover his balance, I pushed him up against the opposite wall of the alley. With his head against the wall, I hit him as hard as I could. With the weight of the quarters in my hand, I heard his jaw shatter. Then two more blows as he started to slide on the wall. I took off his shoes, and using the laces bound his hands and feet.

I took out my cell phone, called Jim Dempsey, and explained the situation. Better the FBI calls the local sheriff than me. I didn't want to take the chance that I'd spend the night in jail, and Miksa released.

They arrived within fifteen minutes and took Miksa into custody to hold for the FBI. It was time for a drink and bed.

Chapter 59

THE NEXT MORNING, I started home. Driving long distances with some Jazz on the radio, I find things bothering me surface, and it becomes clear what I need to do. During the long drive home, it became clear what I needed to do with regards to Cindy O'Brian.

I was nearly home; when I looked at my watch. I picked up my phone off the seat and auto dialed Cindy and put down the phone. Her phone was ringing through the car speakers; then she answered.

"Hello"

"Hello, Cindy, it's Warren."

"What's up."

"I have taken care of my loose ends and called to see if you were free for dinner tonight?"

"That didn't take long. What did you have in mind?"

"I thought I would pick you up and we could have dinner at 'Scotts' in Walnut Creek."

"Oh," was her reply. I think she was thinking Chinese at my house. She went on, "OK. Pick me up at 7:00 tonight?"

"7:00 it is."

I disconnected the phone and continued home.

I arrived at her house just before 7:00. I walked up to the front door and rang the bell, she answered through the intercom.

"It's open, Warren, come in I will be down in just a minute."

I walked in and stood in the living room waiting for her; my mind racing back to times spent here with her. Soon she was coming down the stairs, looking so beautiful. I was beginning to get emotional when she smiled and said, "I'm ready, shall we go?"

I nodded yes, and we left. Not much was said in the car on the way to Scotts. After all, she was living with her ex-husband, who was out of town with their son. This was more than a little uncomfortable for me.

At the restaurant, we quickly ordered, and over two martinis began talking about the Grammys. The excitement of being nominated, the disappointment of losing, etcetera. Then she asked, "I was surprised when you said Maria had gone home that night. Is she OK?"

"She was upset that I went back to get you."

This changed her mood; It sort of lightened up. She reached across the table and took my hands. Looking me in the eyes emotionally, she said, "Warren, when you said to me, you would rather die with me than in the future with cancer, it touched me deeply."

Before she could go on, I stopped her and pulled back my hands . . . I paused, struggling to control my emotions as they rose to choke me. Tears began to form. With moist eyes, I began, "Cindy, I love you as I have never loved anyone, but I need to clear something up . . . I get the feeling you would like for us to be together again. That won't work for me. What we had was so special; it was taken away from us by the stalker. Like Humpty Dumpty, we can never put that back together. We would always be trying to recreate what we had before. It would not work . . . I know I have tried with Maria. She was smart enough to realize before I did that I was trying and hoping I could create what we had but with her. That is why she left."

Her eyes begin to fill with tears.

"We could try, Warren?"

"Nope, I can't. I would always be thinking you were just running from a bad relationship with Rick. Maybe someday our paths will cross, and we will have dealt with all the bad stuff. Maybe then we can fall in love again."

Just then, our dinners came. We sat in silence with nothing more to say; neither of us felt like eating anymore and sort of picked at our food. The waiter came over and asked if everything was OK. I said it was and asked for the check and ordered a taxi for Cindy.

Outside the restaurant, we waited for her taxi. We turned to each other, and we both had tears in our eyes. We started to hug, and Cindy started crying. I held her until she regained her composure. I looked at her and said, "A Grammy nomination; that is something, but I always knew you would make it to the top."

She tilted her head a little to the left, and wiping the tears from her eyes said a quote from

Charles Dickens: "It was the best of times, it was the worst of times."

She then turned and got in the taxi and drove away. I just stood in the damp night watching her leave and thinking,

"As bad as I felt, it might have been better if the terrorist had killed me at the Grammys with his knife."

Three days later, I was on an airplane headed home to Italy. I had some things to take care of at the house. After, I was going to Florence to see Maria. We had talked a few times on the phone, but I needed to see her.

It was Friday; a clear, crisp morning as I drove out of the foothills to the Autostrada and on to Florence. I was driving because I have two book signings, and I was bringing two large boxes full of books. Maria asked if I wanted to stay with her, but I could sense she was just being polite. I said no.

Gazing out the window driving on the autostrada, I started thinking of the events of the last year. It has been a month since the Grammys, and I was still dealing with my emotions surrounding the events. I think of Cindy every day and wonder if that will stop someday: I doubt it. Just then my phone buzzed: Maria

"Ciao, Maria, what's up?"

"Are we still having dinner tonight?"

"Yes."

"The Golden View, say eight o'clock?"

"Perfect, shall I pick you up?"

"No, I will make the reservation, Warren, and meet you there."

"OK."

I took a taxi from my hotel and arrived at the Golden View a little before 8:00 in the evening and walked in and up to the podium.

"May I help you, sir?"

"Yes. Reservations for Sategna?"

He looked down at his list.

"Yes, for two. The other party hasn't arrived yet. I have a nice table with a view of the bridge. Please follow me."

We walked through the restaurant, and I was seated. I asked to have a Bombay martini sent over. He nodded.

"Certainly."

I was looking out the window admiring the view of the Ponte Vecchio when he returned with my martini and Maria. I stood to greet Maria and give her a hug and kisses on both cheeks.

"A cocktail, Maria?"

"No. Just wine with dinner."

We sat and looked at each other for what seemed like an eternity.

Finally, Maria spoke.

"Warren, I want to say how sorry I am to have left you the way I did. I know if it were me instead of Cindy, you would have gone back in, or anybody you knew. I remember the danger you put yourself through for Tom Marino several years back. In fact, every time I see you, you are in danger, protecting someone. I feel awful about leaving you when what you needed the most was to be with someone. I have no excuse for how I acted, but as a way to explain it, I will say this. I became obsessed with the thought of you and her spending eternity together . . . I know it was irrational, and by the time I got home, I felt stupid."

I didn't know how to answer. It was irrational, Maria was right; I did need to be with someone. Where was Cindy? At a post-Grammy party. Where was Maria? On her way home, upset.

"Maria, it was a very emotional time for both of us. Apology accepted; let's forget about it and talk about something else."

She smiled and relaxed. We had a very pleasant dinner and talked about her and my family and our trip down the California coast. After dinner, we walked outside, and I hailed down a Taxi. As it stopped, she asked, "Would you like to come home with me, Warren?"

"Not tonight, I am still working through some emotional issues."

She looked at me and smiled. She understood.

After the book signings were over, I headed home to Muriaglio. I had decided to drop the car, repack, and head to Paris for a month. I was depressed and lonely and felt like shit. Maybe being around people who didn't know my ordeal and did not want to talk about the Grammys would help. Just at that moment, I saw the sign for the turnoff to Lucca. I smiled to myself and took it.

Entering Lucca, I drove straight to Catherina's gallery. I parked in front and went in. She was sitting at a desk doing some paperwork when she heard me come in. She stood and gave me the most welcoming smile: It lit up the whole room.

Walking to me with arms open for a hug, she said, "Warren, it is so good to see you. I was watching the Grammys, and when they started hurrying along with no commercials, I knew something was wrong. Then I chuckled to myself; of course, Warren is there. It is so good of you to come by; sit at this little table, and we will have a wine."

I already felt better; coming was a good decision. We sat and had a wine and talked about the gallery and some of the pieces. Then it came up that I was going to Paris for a month to write some short stories.

"By yourself?"

"That's kind of the plan." Jokingly I continued. "Unless you would like to go."

She lit up.

"Will you wait for me to pack my bag?"

"Of course."

She stood and took our glasses into the back. I sat there, and a quote from Allen Watt came to mind: "I have realized that the past and future are real illusion, that they exist in the present, which is what there is and all there is." Then I laughed to myself. After about five minutes, she returned with a coat on her arm and said, "Let's go. You can take me home. I can pack in ten minutes. I will buy some things in Paris."

I stood, and a little dumbfounded as we headed for the front door asked, "What about the gallery?"

As we went through the front door, she turned the open sign to closed and said, "It will be here when I return." Then looking at me, she said, "Warren, I am a trust fund baby; I have more money than I can ever spend." Then taking me by the arm as we left, she continued, "You can write while I shop for clothes and art for the gallery." Then with an excited little laugh, she said, "Who knows; with some luck, I might end up in a book."

The End